Breaking Boundaries

Copyright

Disclaimer

The books in this series are based completely on dreams that I've had or that one of the other people in my relationship has had. They all have a little bit of real life thrown in so that you, the reader, can get to know us a little bit better.

These books can and should be read as standalone books. There isn't an order to them. All of the characters in the books are the same, as they are all based on characters from real life.

As you read these books, please keep in mind that other than the characters and the city they are based in, these books are not connected to other books in the series. They aren't a continuation of other books. They are all novellas based on dreams that revolve around the same characters.

As you keep that in mind, please enjoy reading this book. I do hope you will also read the others in this series and love them as much as I loved writing them!

Opening Quote

Scars make us who we are. Hearts and homes are broken, broken. Far, we could go so far, with our minds wide open, open. Hey, tears all fall the same. We all feel the rain. We can't change. Everywhere we go, we're looking for the sun. Nowhere to grow old. We're always on the run. They say we'll rot in Hell, but I don't think we will. They've branded us enough. Outlaws of love.

Outlaws Of Love by Adam Lambert

Chapter One

☆ DJ ☆

"Fuck! Are you kidding me? Where the fuck is the flag on that one!" I yell at the TV.

"Are you blind, you fucker?" My best friend, Matt Chance, throws an M&M at the TV. It pings off the screen and goes flying. I'm not sure where.

I take a long drink of my beer and glare at the screen. My beloved Florida Gators are being obliterated by Louisiana State University. But not by any fault of their own. They've had so many penalties called against them during this game that it's comical. But what pisses me off the most are all of the calls that are not called for them. Blatant holds. Personal fouls. Facemasks. Rouging the fucking passer.

"Well, we know who the refs were paid off by," I grumble as I take another drink.

"Yep. Pretty obvious who will be sucking their dicks tonight." Matt gets up and heads for my refrigerator. "Want another beer?"

"Bring the whole fucking case. We're going to need it."

"I prefer my beer cold, Cap."

I grin and shake my head. "Fuck you, Lieutenant."

"Don't tempt me. I haven't had any for longer than I care to admit. My asshole of a Captain put me on a fucking taskforce that keeps me out of my favorite bars at night."

I let out a snort of a laugh. "I'm sure all of Gainesville's female population is thanking me."

"You're such a dick." Matt smiles as he hands me my beer and sits back down.

I laugh because he really isn't wrong. We banter because we're friends, but I'm very much an asshole. I make orders and expect them to be followed. It's part of the reason I'm a Captain with the Gainesville Police Department. I love Florida. I love my job. But I didn't get where I am by being easy-going. I know I demand a lot of my officers. I expect them to give me their best, and be the best.

It's why I get along with Matt so well. He's a Lieutenant with Gainesville Police Department. He was one of my trainees. I trained him, but I didn't have to instill my expectations in him. Matt had the same. He expects the best of himself and everyone else. And he's even his own special brand of asshole.

Lately, though, I think I'm a little too over the top. I'd like to think it's not my fault. I'd like to blame a certain adorable and stupidly beautiful brunette. The fact that she's ignored all of my advances and currently refuses to speak to me has me all turned around.

If I'm being honest, I'm taking my mood out on everyone around me. It's not her fault that I can't seem to get her out of my head. It's mine for falling for a girl I work with who is so far out of my league we aren't even in the same fucking galaxy.

"Oh come on!" I yell at the TV. "He threw him down by his fucking facemask!" I stand and angrily stalk to my kitchen. I yank the refrigerator door open and grab another beer.

"Get me one, too," Matt growls. "I just downed this one."

I grab him one, too, and toss it to him when I sit. "What the hell is happening?" I pop the top on the can and take a long drink.

Matt throws another M&M. "What's happening? What's happening is these fuckers seem to think they need to show the nation who has a bigger set of balls."

I drop my head back and roar with laughter. "I bet you they ain't got fuck behind that zipper."

"Definite compensation. I bet they drive a big ass souped up truck with an illegal lift kit and loud as hell muffler just so they can make themselves look like big men."

I look at him incredulously. "You just bought a brand new F150 and customized it with big tires and a bunch of other shit. Who's compensating?"

He cracks up as he finishes off the beer in literal record time and stands when a commercial comes on. "I guarantee you I ain't got nothing to compensate for." He winks at me and reaches down. He grabs his dick like he's adjusting himself as he laughs and walks towards my kitchen.

He isn't lying, though. He really doesn't have anything to compensate for. I've seen him in all his glory.

I can't help but laugh to myself and shake the image of him out of my head as he disappears behind the refrigerator door. "I'll be honest, Chance. I needed this. Letting loose is the perfect ending to a fucked up week." I sit back and prop my feet up on the coffee table after finishing off my own beer. I count the cans on the table. Four. Nowhere near enough to make me forget her eyes.

Matt sits down again and hands me another can. "You're running out of beer."

"Nah. I have more in the mini-fridge in the den. I don't drink often, but I'm well prepared for when I do."

Matt is quiet for a few minutes before he throws another M&M. "It's like they've totally given up."

"I can't say I wouldn't. Pretty obvious who the refs are calling the game for." I take another drink as a pair of piercing blue eyes cloud my vision. I growl as I glare.

Matt chuckles. "Mariah really got under your skin this time, didn't she?"

I glance at him but don't answer. Instead, I take another drink. It doesn't help, though. Just him saying her name brings her front and center. Like she's standing right in front of me. Close enough to touch.

Closing my eyes doesn't help either. Because then I can see her bent over my desk. Her perky little ass swaying to the music I have playing softly from my phone while she writes me a note. I fight the urge to throw my empty can against a wall.

"How could I have been so fucking stupid?" I grumble. I stand a little too quickly and get slightly dizzy. I ignore it and stumble my way to the kitchen for another beer. I've probably drunk way too much, far too fast, but I don't really care. I'm home. Not going anywhere. I stumble back to the couch and sit down again. I hand Matt another beer.

"What did she do this time?"

I let out a frustrated huff. "You mean other than being hot?" I glance at him before turning back to the game. "Frustratingly beautiful. Ridiculously irresistible."

Matt chuckles. "Sure. Other than that."

I take a slow sip. "This time she didn't do anything. I found her in my office the other day writing me a note. She's taken to writing me cute notes before she heads out on patrol if I'm not in my office. She likes checking in with me and saying good morning."

Matt raises an eyebrow. "So..., you're upset because she's... what? Writing you cute notes and saying good morning? Considering how much I know you like the girl, I wouldn't think that would be a bother."

I huff again and take another drink as I shake my head. Visions of Mariah's ass in her fucking uniform pants overwhelm my damn senses again. And then her piercing blue eyes when she turned them on me. She was pissed, but even then she looked incredible.

Striking.

"No. I'm not upset about that. I know she's been through a lot. I know that despite her turning me down every fucking time I asked her out, that was her way of taking things at her pace. Slow. I'm pissed because of my own fucking mouth."

"Uh oh. Your tongue get you in trouble again?" Matt stands and starts cleaning up the empty cans on the table. He plucks mine out of my hand after I finish it and heads for the kitchen.

"When doesn't it?"

"What did you say to her?"

"I walked in. She was leaning over my desk. She was swaying to a song I had playing on my phone. I'd just come back from grabbing a report from patrol. I said her ass looked good enough to eat. She laughed it off. Then I touched her lower back and told her my desk would look better with her on it naked and spread open for me."

Matt's mouth drops. "You fucking didn't."

I nod. "I did. Realized what a colossal fuck up that was when she slowly stood up and turned to me. Slapped me across the face. Hard. Then very calmly and beyond angrily walked out of my office. I didn't even try to block the slap or make a move to stop her from walking out."

"Jesus Christ. Were you fucking drunk?"

I shake my head slowly. "Nope." I take a long drink of the beer, downing half the can. "But I'm about to be."

"Do you have any idea how long it took me to get her on my desk? Months, DJ. And she still won't fuck me. You need to apologize." He focuses back on the TV and takes a drink of his own beer.

"I've tried. Several times. She refuses to talk to me. I can't blame her. She won't even answer me on the radio. Yesterday, I called her because I needed her to follow up on a call. She had Lyric answer the radio for her."

Matt chuckles. "I heard that. I wondered what that was about. It doesn't matter. If you like her, you need to talk to her. And I told you before. I'll back off if that's what you want. Even though I know she's insanely attracted to me." He gives me a teasing smile.

I shake my head and chuckle. "Ain't like we ain't shared before. But I told you. It's her call. I'm not going to force her to choose between us. I already know she likes us both."

"Yeah. Because I told you." He takes another drink. "You need to talk to her."

"There's no coming back from this one." I down the rest of my beer and focus back on the screen. "Much like this game."

"Yeah, I don't think the Gators are going to be winning this one."

"Not a fucking chance." I stand and stumble a little on my way to the kitchen. I grab a large bowl and drop the last of the cans in it. I fill it with ice. I take it and the two cans of beer in my hand back to the couch.

Matt pops a couple of M&M's in his mouth as I sit. "Good idea. I didn't want to get back up." He takes the can I hand him and nods towards the TV. "Another fucking holding. I didn't see it."

I shake my head. "Probably because it wasn't there. Pretty sure the refs are just trying to prove who has a bigger dick at this point. What's up with you and Lyric? Get my mind off Mariah."

He chuckles. "I swear that girl wants nothing to do with me."

I raise an eyebrow and glance at him. "You know that's not true."

His chuckle turns into a full laugh. "I don't know what you thought you heard the last time your head was between her legs, but it was not my fucking name. Yesterday, she told me she couldn't wait to break me as low as I make her feel. I can't make sense of my feelings for Mariah. Add Lyric into it, and I'm a fucking mess."

I open my beer, then tap mine to his in a toast. "Welcome to the club. Cheers."

"You and I are two very fucked up people." Matt is starting to slur.

I just nod. I have a very nice buzz going on right now. Everything is starting to get a little fuzzy. I grab a handful of popcorn and reach over to the bowl Matt has between his legs. My hand brushes against the zipper of his jeans as I grab a few M&M's.

"Fuck. I'm sorry." I'm getting drunker, but definitely not enough to not have noticed his dick twitch when it happened. It's not like we haven't been together before. But there was always a girl between us.

He glances at me and puts his feet up on the table. "Not worried about it." He takes a drink as he shakes his head. "This game is bullshit."

"You're telling me." I lean back and kick my feet back up on the table. I rest my thigh against Matt's, but I'm not sure when we got close enough on this couch for that to happen.

It doesn't really matter to me. The alcohol is finally making me numb. I don't want to move. Judging that he hasn't moved, I don't think he gives a shit either. I eat my popcorn with the M&M's and continue watching the absolute demise of the University of Florida Gators. Every time they make up ground, they get some bullshit penalty called against them. I've seen maybe one the entire game that they've actually deserved.

By the time the second half starts, my mood has vastly improved. Mariah and her sexy as sin smile is far away in the dark corners of my mind. The alcohol has warmed my blood. Matt's laugh has made me feel lighter.

"Look at the coach's face. He looks like he's about to murder this ref. Fuck, if I were the QB, I'd fire one right at the ref's balls. *Longest Yard* style."

I laugh. "I haven't seen that movie in a long time." I reach down and adjust myself. There are a lot of blessings in having a large dick like I do. But it comes with a price. It doesn't matter if I'm erect or not. My dick has a habit of making things uncomfortable.

"Fuck," Matt grumbles. I glance over and see him adjusting himself, too.

I chuckle. "Issue?"

"Yeah. Jeans can be a little restricting when you have something to be proud of hanging between your legs."

"Don't I know it. More than I can say for those fuckers."

Matt laughs. "At least I don't have anything to compensate for."

"Can't complain myself." I don't know why I bothered saying that. I know he knows.

Matt glances at me. I don't know if it's the beer or the intense stare he's giving me, but I can't help but look back. His eyes aren't focused on me, though. At least not on my face. He's fixated on my dick, which causes me to look directly at his.

Matt has a very nice dick. I can see the outline of it hanging down his inner right thigh. It looks much better when it's not being hidden.

I shake my head and quickly snap my eyes back to the game. Of all things I could be thinking, how long it's been since I've had Matt's dick in my hand really shouldn't be one of them. Matt grabs another beer, handing me one as well. Fucking good thing because my throat is suddenly very dry.

"How big are you?"

I cough and sputter. "What?"

Matt laughs. "I mean, I've seen it. But I've never actually asked. I'm proud to say I was always the biggest one in the locker room. My teammates hated me. I had my pick of anyone I wanted. Male or female."

I laugh. "You know, one thing I've always liked about you is that you don't hold back." I look over at him with a smirk. "Nine inches."

His smile grows. "Ten."

My eyes widen. "Bullshit. It doesn't look that big."

He holds up his hands and looks at his dick where my eyes have fallen once more. "Swear."

I laugh again. "What the fuck is this? High school? Comparing dick sizes?"

He smiles at me and settles back into the couch. He rests his hand on his dick and focuses back on the screen. "If this were high school, we'd have them out right now having a show and tell."

I grin and settle back as well. I rest my thigh against his again. "Having a Star Wars like lightsaber fight with our dicks." I reach down and mimic grabbing mine. I make lightsaber noises while moving my hips side to side like I'm having a real fight with it. I know it looks ridiculous, but I'm too drunk to give a single fuck.

Matt groans about a second before his lips are on mine. My heart hammers in my chest, but I plunge my tongue into his mouth, giving him a groan of my own. His fingers spear my hair as he deepens the kiss. His tongue plunges into my mouth and starts a fucking war. I suck his. He nips mine.

Before I know what's happening, I'm pushing him off me. We're both panting. He looks at me like he's about to apologize. We've both been with men and women. We've been with each other. But never alone like this. We've always had a girl between us that our attention was focused on. Not to say we've never touched each other. We have. But not like this.

I shift and plunge my tongue back into his mouth again and again. Our battle starts once more, only slightly reversed. He moans into the kiss and sucks on my tongue. His nails dig into my back. I nip his tongue and tug his hair. My other hand splays across his abs. I grip his shirt.

"Oh fuck," Matt moans. His hot and hungry mouth blazes down to my neck. He sucks and bites it. He scrapes his teeth across my throat.

I tug at his jeans. "Jesus Christ."

Matt grips my ass and growls as he practically shoves me back on the couch. My leg hits the table and sends the bowl of popcorn flying. But all I can think about is how Matt feels in my hand. How much I've missed it. He's a big guy. Something like six feet four. He's very well-built. He spends time in the gym, but not so much that his muscles look fake. Matt is all natural.

All very much natural.

The size of his dick and all. It's long. Thick. Maybe not as thick as mine, but thick enough that he definitely has nothing to be ashamed of. His stubble against my neck makes me moan, but it's when his hand finds my dick that I arch.

It's been too long. Being with a man or woman. Him. Way too fucking long. Maybe it's the alcohol talking. Maybe it's my libido. Maybe it's the fact that my blood feels like it's on fire. Despite the fact that we've done it before, fucking around with my best friend feels exactly as it should. A little dangerous. A little wrong. But fucking perfect.

It's because it feels so familiar that I start undoing his belt with one hand and scratching my nails up his back with the other. I find the button and pop it. He reaches down and holds himself down while I unzip him. I push his jeans down while he kisses me long and hard. Demandingly. So fucking demandingly it makes me want to slap his ass and take back the control he's trying to take from me.

But Matt is faster than me. Not by much, but enough that instead of slapping his ass like I want to, I'm gripping his ass and digging my nails in while he slams his dick in my ass. My head drops back onto the couch. My eyes roll back in my head as I close them.

This…

This is new. We've never done this with each other before.

"Shit. Holy shit, Matt." My ass clenches hard around him. I haven't been with anyone in too long. Way too long. But it feels different with Matt then it ever has with anyone I've ever been with. It's like he belongs with me. Just like this. It feels so good that all I want to do is relish the feeling. He doesn't give me that option though.

Matt grips my thigh with one hand and angles me so he slides deeper into me as he thrusts. "My God. If I'd known it would be this good, I wouldn't have waited."

The statement makes me laugh, but it turns into a deep moan as I meet his hard and punishing thrusts. "You telling me you'd have bent me over my desk?"

"Fuck no. Over mine," he growls against my neck.

"God. Fuck." I clench around him and keep meeting every thrust he slams into me. I grip his ass harder and pull him into me. I bite his shoulder when he bites mine.

The thought of being bent over his desk brings a very fuzzy image to the forefront of my mind, but I'm too drunk and high on Matt fucking Chance to bother to focus more on it. Matt is intoxicating. His muscles working against mine as he pumps his dick harder and harder into my ass is the best feeling in the world to me right now.

At this moment in time, we're just two people in the world giving each other the release we desperately need. Chasing that release is all that matters to me. That's how fucking good he feels pounding into me.

"Holy fuck, I'm gonna come," Matt moans into my neck.

"I'll let you as long as you get me there." I scratch my nails up his back.

He arches and closes his eyes. He comes deep in my ass. "Holy fuck, DJ!" His hips jerk as jet after jet of come fills me. When he finally stops, he collapses against me. "Fuck."

I'm not the kind of guy who would ever not let my sexual partner come down after an intense orgasm like that. I'm almost fifty-years-old. I've learned a few things over the years. Which is why I put my needs in this moment aside and run my hands up and down Matt's back as he comes down instead of taking him like I want to.

"Doing okay?" I ask quietly.

"I don't know where the fuck that came from," he mumbles into my neck. He slowly pulls out and pushes himself up.

I give him a wicked grin as I slowly follow. "Obviously something you needed."

Our jeans and underwear are still at our knees. But it's the least of my concerns as I stand. I let them fall as I lean down and kiss him. Still on his knees, he reaches up and tangles his fingers in my short dark hair. He tugs and moans when I deepen the kiss.

I pull away slowly and guide him so he's facing the back of the couch. But being slow is not at all how I want this to go. I slam into his ass just as hard and deeply as he did me. He grips the couch and pushes his ass back into me as he clenches around my dick.

He drops his head and moans. "Fuck. Yes." He reaches his hand back and grips my thigh when I start thrusting into him.

I lean into his back and wrap one arm around his waist; the other around his chest. I lean my head down and bury my face into his neck. I kiss it and thrust hard and deep, gradually picking up speed until I'm slamming deep, fast, and hard into him while I'm slamming him into the couch.

"Fucking hell, Matt." I bite his shoulder and scrape my teeth along it.

"That's where we'll be going, I'm sure, but I'm too fucked up to care." He turns his head and kisses me as he pushes back into me hard, making me slam deeper into him.

He clenches around me with every thrust, digging his nails into my thigh as he pulls me into him. The alcohol in my system starts to slosh around in my stomach just as my spine begins to tingle as I near my release. I ignore my stomach with a growl and bury myself in Matt.

"No one should feel as good as you," I slur in his ear, no longer really having an idea what I'm saying. I give into the feel of him and nothing more. I come hard as I collapse against him, pressing him against the couch.

"Maybe it's the alcohol, but I'm fucking spent," Matt says. "Damn close to passing out."

I kiss his neck softly. "Clean up first. Then pass out." I pull out gently and help him up.

How we get upstairs and cleaned up, though, is something I'm not totally sure I understand.

After it's done, we fall into bed. I vaguely feel him against me before I pass out into a blessed, hazy darkness.

Chapter Two

★ Lyric ★

"So, wait," my best friend and fellow police officer, Mariah Carter, says to me as we watch the TV in our living room. "Why? You always feel ridiculous after you do that. Used and…" She waves her hand like she has no idea of the words. But I know better. I know exactly what she wants to say.

I sigh. "Used and worthless. Like the rest of DJ's conquests." I play with my fingers.

"Flag on the play. Take a drink."

I glance at the screen. "What just happened?" I take a drink.

"Florida just had another holding penalty called on them." Mariah shakes her head. "I swear the refs are doing it on purpose."

We're watching our local college football team, the Florida Gators, lose miserably to Louisiana State University. And playing a drinking game. Every time something bad happens, we drink. I don't know much about American football. I'm from the United Kingdom. I've lived here for a few years and work for the Gainesville Police Department alongside Mariah. I'm following all of my dreams. I've always wanted to live in America. Florida to be exact. And I've always wanted to be a cop.

Meeting Mariah in our training class was the blessing I never knew I needed. We quickly became best friends and decided to room with each other when we decided where we lived wasn't the right place for us. We both had an apartment near the University and hated it. It was noisy and very sketchy. But it was when I saw a drug deal go down right in front of me in the hallway of my building that I decided I wanted out.

Lucky for me, Mariah was also in the market for a new place and wanting to live in a better area. Being flashed by a man in the building she lived in while she was unlocking her door is definitely a good reason to want to move.

I turn my cup in my hands, already feeling a little wasted. Good. I need it. Maybe it will get the dark brown eyes and brooding Lieutenant out of my head. Tall, dark, and handsome. It describes Matt Chance perfectly.

"I hate him," I grumble.

Mariah chuckles. "Are we still talking about the Captain whose tongue you have an obsession with?"

I look at her and laugh. "No. Though, I hate him, too."

She smiles softly. "You don't hate DJ. You hate how you feel after."

"Just another girl in the line of many."

"Another drink. Personal foul," Mariah says quietly.

I do as I'm told. Anything to drown my dilemma. I nibble on a Dorito as I stare blankly at the TV and sigh as I ponder. I have really, really liked my Lieutenant for a long while. Matt Chance is truly a great guy. My problem is that I don't know what to make of him. He's such a player. I know he spends a lot of time wooing Gainesville's single ladies. I've even seen him with men.

He's the definition of man whore if there ever was one. He's not a safe bet. All women want safety when it comes to relationships. Hell. All men want the same thing. Whether they admit it or not. I've tried to convince myself that he just hasn't found what he's looking for. Or that maybe he just doesn't know. But the guy is forty years old. He's ten years older than me.

I have to laugh a little and shake my head. Who am I kidding? I don't have my ducks in a row. Not even a little. I'm a mess. I can't decipher my feelings for anything. Which is probably why I've done all I can to stay away from Matt. We're both a disaster waiting to happen.

"Drink," Mariah sighs. "Stupid holdings. Gators aren't winning this game."

I chuckle as I drink. Mariah loves her football. She lives and breathes for the University of Florida Gators and the Tampa Bay Buccaneers during football season. She doesn't miss a game. Ever. When the season is over, she sulks for two weeks. Almost like she's in mourning or something. It's one of the most adorable things I've ever seen.

Today, she's decided we both need a time out from the week we've had. It's been a long one. I want nothing more than to forget it. Drowning in alcohol while watching a game I don't fully understand seems like the best option. And I was definitely not wrong. The shots are doing their job.

Not fast enough, though. I figure as long as I can still see Matt's sexy as sin smile and his beautiful dark brown eyes, it means I haven't drank near enough. As long as the tattoos covering his arms are still visible to me, I'll need more to drink.

Thank God, the Gators aren't disappointing. I chuckle when another flag is thrown against them. "Drink."

Mariah grumbles. "I have to wonder if this game is fixed." She tosses back her shot and coughs. "Gross."

I laugh. "You're the one who decided this was a good idea."

She smiles and points at me teasingly. "As my friend, you should have stopped me, and reminded me that I hate the taste of alcohol."

I crack up. "Next time."

She shakes her head. "There will not be a next time."

I bite my lip and look at her teasingly. "Sure. Just like there won't be a next time with me and DJ and his magical tongue. Even though I feel like shit afterwards."

She tries not to smile but can't. "See? That's the whole reason I refuse to have anything to do with him and his advances. He's a playboy."

"And Matt isn't?" I know I have her when she lowers her eyes, but I instantly regret the words. "Shit. I'm sorry." I scoot closer and hug her when I cuddle into her side.

It takes her a while to say anything, but after a couple more bad calls and downed shots, she looks at me. "What is wrong with me?"

I smile softly and run my fingers through her hair. "Nothing. You're entitled to have fun after the marriage you came out of." I lean my head on her shoulder.

"I feel like a slut," she says quietly.

"Good Christ, you're the farthest thing from it." I keep running my fingers soothingly through her hair. Sometimes, it's the only thing that really relaxes her.

"To willingly fuck around with one man while pining for another after having sexual relations with my roommate is definitely my own special kind of crazy," she whispers with a sniffle.

I smile to myself at her slurred words. She's definitely hit the nail on the head. "Well, I know Matt likes you. And we know you like him. Or at least his fingers. And tongue."

I focus back on the screen when she chuckles. I take a breath. When I really think about it, even I know how out of this world ridiculous our lives are. Mariah has had a type of relationship with our Lieutenant for a long time. They started as really good friends. It flourished into something not quite an actual relationship, but more than just friends. It's almost like a friends with benefits thing. I really didn't know that existed until them.

But she also has very strong feelings towards our Captain, DJ Rens. She's friends with him. She talks to him. At least she did until a couple of days ago when he said something stupid. She won't tell me what it was, but it pissed her off. And it hurt her, too, because even hearing his voice makes her tear up.

It's not lost on me that I sort of have the same type of relationships as her. Opposite of her, but the same. I became almost instant friends with DJ. We ended up in this very strange friends with benefits thing, too. The only difference is, I have feelings for DJ. Strong feelings for him. I don't know that Mariah has strong feelings for Matt or if he just makes the hurt go away for a few minutes.

I, on the other hand, do have strong feelings for Matt. It's the entire reason I'm trying to stay far away from him. It's too dramatic. Having feelings like I do for DJ, but also having them for Matt makes me feel awful. And every time I slip up and express my feelings for DJ, I feel great during the moment. When it's over though, I feel exactly as Mariah does. A little dirty.

The other part of me, though, feels right. Like I'm doing exactly what I'm supposed to. It's a complicated life I lead. A very long walk on a freakishly thin tightrope. I second guess myself all the time when it comes to them.

Mariah and I take comfort in each other. Mostly, just like this. Watching a movie or game. We talk. We know more about each other than anyone else does in our lives. She knows about my feelings for Matt and DJ and how conflicting they are. I know about her feelings for them, too, and exactly how it makes her feel.

"I can't watch this game anymore," Mariah slurs. "I'm going to get alcohol poisoning."

I chuckle and lean forward to put the cap back on the bottle. "Not much left." I drink the last bit of it and savor the burn of it going down my throat.

Mariah looks at the TV disgusted and shakes her head. She reaches for her water. "How dumb is it that we have the hots for the same guys and don't hate each other?"

"Diabolically crazy." I lean my head back on the couch as Mariah lays her head in my lap.

One of my favorite things to do is play with Mariah's hair. I love that it's also one of her favorite things. She loves feeling my fingers running through it. I love that she does the same thing for me when I need it or want it.

"I think it's one of the things that bothers me the most about this whole..." She waves her hand in front of her but doesn't finish.

I don't say anything, but I do smile softly. Mariah thinks and overthinks. Then she thinks some more. It's another thing we have in common. Truthfully, it's something I don't really understand myself. What kind of women openly talk about how much they want a guy that the other has openly talked about her sex life with?

"You'd think I'd feel drunker than I am," I say quietly.

"Oh, give it a few minutes. The longer you let it seep into your bloodstream, the more drunk you'll feel. Soon you won't remember your name."

I giggle. "Mariah."

"Who's Mariah?" she mumbles against my stomach as she turns around and closes her eyes.

I look down and laugh. She smiles and burrows. She shifts and wraps her arms around me, then buries her face between my legs. I bite back a moan and keep running my fingers through her hair. I don't doubt that while she could take care of the tingling between my thighs always caused by thoughts of Matt, I also think she'll pass out in mere minutes. So I force myself to stay still and let her relax.

After a few minutes, I close my eyes as I feel the alcohol finally do what I had been hoping it would. It gradually erases Matt from my mind. It shoves him back to the deep abyss where he belongs. I finally feel myself relaxing after the long week we've had.

It takes me a few minutes to realize that Mariah is giggling. I look down at her seconds before I feel her pulling my panties aside and kitten licking my clit. Easy access since we are both only wearing Gator jerseys and panties. The reaction to her is instant. My pussy clenches and tightens. I feel the familiar warmth start seeping through me.

I tighten my grip on her hair. "Oh, holy fuck." I arch into her.

"Mmm… This is much better than that game." She nips my clit, setting me on fire.

I drop my head back and moan. I jerk my hips against her tongue and pull her closer to my pussy. I need more pressure, but also want her tongue buried in me. She knows exactly how to make me forget any kind of nonsense floating around in my head. She knows I love DJ's tongue, but secretly I just may love hers more.

"Oh my fuck!" I shout when she drives two fingers deep into my pussy at the same time she sucks my clit into her mouth.

"Yummy…"

She thrusts hard and as deep as she can, burying her fingers in my pussy. I pulse and clench around her fingers while my hips jerk into her tongue along to the rhythm of her fingers. I grab her wrist and tug her hair as my thighs tremble.

"Oh my God, Mariah!"

She giggles against my clit, then moans. She pulls her fingers out of my pussy slowly, making me whimper at the loss. But she doesn't make me wait. She plunges her tongue into me with a groan. She shifts and sets her thumb against my clit. I don't know how she does it, but she knows just how much pressure to give me as she rubs in a slow circle.

Her tongue is darting in and out of my pussy rapidly. The stark difference between her tongue and thumb is sending my mind into a frenzy of pure bliss. I can't think. All I can do is feel and ride her tongue.

She sucks hard on my pussy and flicks my clit. "Mmm... Lyric," she slurs.

The edges of my vision darken, but I don't know if it's because I'm drunk or if it's her. "Yes. Yes!"

My pussy pulses uncontrollably for her. My entire body trembles. I tug her closer. She buries her tongue deeper and moans low, sending vibrations straight to every spot in my body that brings any kind of pleasure. I feel like I'm tingling down to my toes. I'm thrashing against her, silently begging her for release.

She sucks on my pussy as she twirls her tongue. "Come for me," she whispers. Somehow the feel of her breath against me as she pinches my clit sends me further over the edge.

I scream. "Mariah! Yes! Yes! Oh my fuck. Yes!" I buck up into her and come hard, soaking her tongue and probably her face.

She grips my ass and digs her nails in as she starts licking everything I give her. "So sexy..." she slurs while she licks me clean, simultaneously helping me to come down.

I moan. "Fucking hell, Mariah. Oh my God." My grip on her hair loosens as she slowly sits up, licking her lips. I can't resist crushing my lips to hers. Tasting myself on her tongue is everything. She tastes so sweet. Mixed with my tangy taste, and I'm begging for her lips.

I push her back on the couch. After tasting me on her sweet lips, I can't think of anything right now but tasting her. Maybe it's the fact that the alcohol has finally done what it was intended to. I'm very nicely wasted. Thoughts of anything other than the woman in front of me are long gone.

I nip her thigh and smile when she giggles. I want to tease her a little, but I don't think I can. I just want her taste on my tongue. I pull her panties aside and dive in without a second thought. I roughly lick her pussy and shake my head back and forth as I swirl my tongue.

"Holy fuck, Lyric!" She grips my hair and arches off the couch.

I grab her ass and squeeze, licking her pussy relentlessly. I nip and suck my way up to her clit as she writhes and moans underneath me. I suck her clit into my mouth hard, flicking it around quickly with my tongue as I give her low moans. I know I'm sending vibrations directly through her clit.

"Mmm…," I moan again before thrusting my tongue back into her pussy. I thrust hard and as deeply as I can. I use my grip on her ass to pull her into my tongue.

"Oh God. Oh God!" She grips the couch cushion with her other hand and pulls me closer.

I feel her start to tremble and shudder beneath as she climbs the hill to her release. Her pussy clenches and pulses hard around me before she finally clamps down on my tongue. I scrape my teeth lightly along her clit when I open my mouth wider.

She begins quivering erratically and closes her legs around my shoulders. Not enough to squeeze me, but enough to make her tighter for me. I keep licking, enjoying her taste. I shake my head back and forth again, making my tongue twirl inside her and her clamp harder around it.

"Mmm… Come, Rih."

She screams and arches her hips forward. "Holy… Oh! Oh! God, yes! Lyric!" She jerks with the force of her release and spills everything I want from her onto my tongue.

Giving her the same treatment she did me, I slowly lick her clean as I help her to come down. She pants and moans quietly. I look up at her, but I don't need to in order to know she has a dazed look on her face. It's the same that's on mine.

I stand slowly. The blood rushes to my head. I sway. "Oh… wow…," I mutter.

"Are you okay?" Mariah asks quietly.

"You were right. Delayed reaction. Alcohol has definitely kicked in." I look at the mess we've made on the table.

Mariah groans and slowly sits up, holding her head. "That was a terrible idea."

She's looking at the table. It's a mess. Somewhere in my haste to taste her, I knocked over the chips. How they got wet, though, I don't really know. I give her a soft smile, but she doesn't look up at me. She starts to slowly clean up, though she's fighting the alcohol.

I bite my lip and quietly start to help her, sobering up far more quickly than I'd like to. I'd hoped to be passed out cold by the time

Mariah's guilt set in. It always makes me feel so much worse about our situation.

I've been very open about who I am. I'm not ashamed of it or afraid of it. I'm attracted very much to both men and women. Well, rather just one woman. I've never been attracted to another woman, really. Just Mariah. I'm pansexual and beyond proud of it.

Mariah, on the other hand, isn't open about her sexuality in the slightest. In fact, while she enjoys the moment as much as I do, when it's over, she becomes withdrawn. I know it's because she's afraid of the fact that she liked it. But I hate seeing her so guilty over it.

It's the reason that her statement about it being a terrible idea cuts me as much as it does. I know she's talking about what happened between us. Though, she'd have me believe she was referring to the mess.

It's just one more thing that makes my life far more complicated. I'm hopelessly attracted to three people.

And I have no idea just what in the hell to do about it.

Chapter Three

☆ Matt ☆

I tap my foot against the floor and make a valiant attempt at focusing on the reports in front of me. But my mind isn't up for the task. The only thing I have is that there were a lot of calls. We were fully staffed. And three of our cops took a very disproportionate amount of calls compared to the others. Other than that, I have no idea what the hell I'm looking at.

I growl at the screen, though it really isn't the computer's fault. It's mine and my sudden inability to put my life aside and keep my heart out of my fucking hook-ups. I haven't had an issue with it for forty years. Compartmentalizing is my specialty.

Unfortunately for me, that doesn't seem to be the case anymore. I'd blame DJ, but even I know that isn't who is at fault. This is all on me. I allowed myself to catch feelings for someone I don't have business to feel anything for.

DJ and I have spent a few nights together. But not once, other than a hand job, kissing, and some heavy petting, did we allow ourselves to really get sexual with each other. Not like last night. And not once did we ever wake up wrapped in each other's fucking arms.

It was such a shock that we both almost fell off the bed when we jumped away from each other. We stared at each other for a full minute trying to catch our breath before either of us dared say a word.

And it was the words that had managed to make my head spin, my heart hurt, and my hangover way worse than it should be. They put me in a foul mood, but only because I can't figure out what the hell I want to do about them.

We had decided to take a shower. I think it was more to cool off and gather ourselves. After he was finished and I'd taken mine, DJ said he thought it was a good idea to forget it happened. And like a stupid fucking idiot, I agreed.

The truth is, I don't want to forget about it. I don't know how to make sense of it, but I sure as hell don't want to forget about it. I didn't want to continue the conversation with him. The words he'd uttered sort of felt like a gunshot to the stomach. So I let him leave. I didn't tell him that I have feelings for him. I probably have for a long time. I'm sure it's the only reason that of all my sexual partners, he's the only one that I've been with more than once.

Well, other than Mariah. And it's because I have feelings for her, too. It's not just a friends with benefits relationship to me. I really like her. I have for a long time. I just haven't told her because I don't think she feels that way about me. DJ on the other hand, I'm pretty sure she'd fall at his feet. Regardless of how upset she is with him right now.

Add in Lyric and the way I feel about her, even though I am not her favorite person, and I lead one hell of a fucked up life. Very strong feelings for three different people. How the fuck did I allow this to happen?

I let out another low and angry growl at myself just as my office door quietly opens. It shuts just as quietly after a beautiful, petite brunette sneaks through it. She doesn't say anything. I'm not totally sure she's even breathing. Not until she leans her head against the door and lets out a long breath.

I smile and look at her from the top of her head down to her toes. Mariah Carter is definitely the highlight of my morning. "Want to tell me why you're not in uniform, officer?" I lean back in my chair with a teasing smile.

She doesn't turn around. She stays still in her tiny shorts and tank top. "It happened again." She says it so quietly, I have to strain to hear her.

"Oh, baby."

She lets out another long breath and keeps her head against the door. "I cried the whole morning."

I let out a quiet sigh and stand. She doesn't need to tell me what it is she's talking about. This happens every time she slips and ends up fucking around with her roommate, Lyric. The same Lyric I have my own thing for. It's like our own fucked up foursome.

When I get to her, I reach around her and lock my office door. I wrap my arms around her and pull her back into my chest. I hug her tightly, resting my chin on her head. I don't have to stoop or strain to do it. Mariah is around a foot shorter than me and half my size, but she fits perfectly.

She's a very small girl. Shy as hell and very self-conscious about the size of her tits in proportion to the rest of her body. They're large. Unless she's wearing a hoodie, she shows cleavage. Which is the reason she always wears a black Under Armour t-shirt underneath her uniform shirt. A lot of girls wear a tank top or something. Not Mariah.

She turns in my arms and wraps around me, resting her arm on the butt of my gun. "Why do I do this to myself?"

"Do you really want me to answer that?" I sway gently with her.

"No… Yes… Maybe…" She shakes her head. "No."

I chuckle softly. "You know I'm going to, though."

I feel her deflate. "Yes…"

"Rih, you're pansexual. There's nothing wrong with it. I am. You know that. You know Lyric is. DJ is. You know that, baby."

"I can't be…"

I raise an eyebrow but keep her in my arms. "Can't?"

She shakes her head. "My family would disown me." It's a good thing I have good hearing. If I didn't, I'd never be able to hear her because of how quietly she's talking.

"Honey, I don't know if you remember or not, but you haven't spoken to anyone in your family since you moved here four years ago."

She sniffles. "I still talk to them sometimes. Just not a lot or for long."

"Okay. I'll concede to that. Not including your aunt because I know she'll accept you, and I know you like talking to her, you feel like shit after talking to anyone else. And I always end up holding you just like this for hours afterwards. Do you really give a shit what your family thinks? Honestly? Or do you think maybe you should stop letting them make you feel like you're nothing and start living your own life?"

"It's not that easy for me, Matt." She pulls away and wipes her eyes. I let her go and watch her as she walks to the chairs in front of my desk. She doesn't sit. Instead, she turns back to me. "I grew up believing that it's wrong. So, so wrong. That it's a sin to have feelings for someone of the same sex. People condemned my cousin for being gay. Not... counting my aunt. Or grandmother. Or uncle. Everyone else, though?"

"But, honey, you have feelings for someone of the same sex. Does that make you a bad person?"

She looks down at the floor as she leans against my desk. "I've never thought it was wrong for someone to love someone of the same sex."

I walk slowly towards her. I tilt her chin up slowly so she's looking at me when I stand in front of her. "So, it's not wrong for, say, me and DJ to fuck around or be in a relationship. But for some reason it is for you? It makes you a bad person, but not me? Not DJ? Not Lyric?"

Her beautiful blue eyes fill with tears as she shakes her head. "No... I..." She sniffles. "I don't know."

"Honey, I get the feeling there's a lot more to this than what you're telling me."

Something flashes in her eyes that I can't quite read. She pulls away again and looks down. "I'm just confused."

I watch her for a few moments before taking a step back. I kiss the top of her head and walk to my chair. I have to put some distance between me and her coconut infused hair before I make everything worse for both of us. I'm already trying to decipher feelings. I need to take the time to do that before I start anything with anyone. Even if I have technically started something with her already.

"You're not going to be able to unconfuse yourself until you fully admit to yourself who you are, Mariah. You're almost forty. It's time you start living for yourself." I stare at her back, waiting.

I know my girl. I know what's coming. She's good at fighting it, but pretty soon she'll start crying. And I won't be able to handle that. I can't stand seeing her cry. She's been through enough. Seeing her torture herself kills me every fucking time. I don't know if being with me really helps her or not, but for a little while, she forgets. She smiles. She's Mariah again.

I know it will fuck me up, but I don't care. All I care about is her. I can't force her to admit to herself that she's pansexual, but if I can at least do something to center her again, even if it's only for a while, I'll do it. I don't care that it's a vicious circle. I can't handle her pain.

Just as I knew she would, Mariah covers her beautiful face with her hands and breaks down. "What's wrong with me? Why am I like this? How can I be in love with three people?"

The declaration is like a sucker punch to my balls. My eyes widen. I suck in a breath. I'd always thought she just used me for some kind of a release. I'd never asked for anything from her in return, even though she's definitely given me just as much as I have her. It's unlike me in every possible way. I'd always just been happy to be whatever it was that she needed and hope that maybe one day we'd get past this partial thing we have.

Her admission blows me away. Her tears, though. Those, as usual, hurt me. So, against my better judgment, I go to her. I pull her trembling body into my arms and guide her around my desk. I sit in my chair and pull her into my lap. It's going to kill me, but I can't do what she's going to ask me to. I thought I could. But I can't. I can't. Not this time. Not after what she just said.

"Make me forget, Matt. Please," she whispers as she chokes on a sob.

It takes everything I am to shake my head into her neck and kiss it as I hug her as tightly as I dare. "No, honey. Not this time. Not that I don't want to, but it's not what you need this time." I expect her to argue. I don't expect her to cry harder. "Jesus." I tangle my fingers in her hair and hold her tighter.

"O-two-x to squad twelve," a growly voice says over the radio.

Mariah grips me tighter. "I can't answer that." She takes a deep breath, but coughs into my shoulder.

I rub one hand up and down her back as I answer the radio with the other. "Twenty-seven to O-two-x. Twelve is otherwise engaged. She'll be on patrol when I'm done with her."

"We're short out here, Lieutenant," the growly Sergeant responds. "I need my cops out here."

I kiss Mariah's neck before responding. Because if I don't, I'll snap. "And I said I need her. I'll give her to you when I'm through with her."

He mumbles something as Mariah nuzzles my neck. She sits up and wipes her eyes. I keep my arm firmly around her because I don't trust that she's ready for me to let go. After a few moments of composing herself, she gives me a weak smile. I reach up and wipe her eyes with my thumb because I can't resist touching her.

"Thank you," Mariah says with another sniffle.

"I don't need a thank you, honey."

She chuckles and nods. "Yes. You really do. You knew what I needed. Even when I didn't."

I lean in and kiss her forehead. "Always. You okay to head out there? Or do you want me to take a couple hours so you can get dressed and not worry about Sergeant Jackson?"

"I'll have to deal with him anyway," she says quietly. She shakes her head. "Sometimes, I think he has it out for me."

"I've told you just say the word, Rih." I kiss her cheek. "He keeps fucking with you, he'll deal with me."

She giggles, successfully putting my heart back together from the tears that shattered it. "That's why I haven't told you."

I laugh. "You're no fun."

She smiles. "Maybe you could take a couple of hours? I don't mean to ask for special treatment just because -"

"Mariah. Enough. You know I'm happy to do it. I don't get out there as much as I'd like to. If it weren't for the taskforce Rens put us on, I probably wouldn't get out there at all. Now go get dressed. You shouldn't have to deal with anyone. They're all out there already."

I know she knows who I mean. I don't say Lyric's name because I don't want to upset her again. Judging from the small smile she gives me, I know the decision was the right one.

She gives me a soft kiss on the corner of the mouth as she gets up. "You're truly amazing."

"Don't let that get around." I smile teasingly.

"Wouldn't dream of it." She gives me another smile as she heads for the door.

I wait a few minutes as I compose myself. Saying no to having my head between Mariah's thighs is yet one more thing not typical of me. Lately, that's all I've been doing. A non-typical thing followed by some other action I don't do. Ever.

I scrub my hands down my face as I get up. I grab my keys and head for the garage. I look around for the squad I usually drive. It's not where I left it. I don't drive any other squad. Everyone who works here knows that.

My eyes fall on Sergeant Jackson. I glare. "Jackson!"

He jumps and drops his clipboard. "Fucking hell, Chance. What the fuck?" He bends his pudgy ass over to pick up his clipboard but can't reach it. He kneels instead, nearly falling on his face.

He's on the other side of the garage by the entrance, but I stride over there before he's standing again. "Where's my squad?"

He looks at me slightly hesitantly before looking down at his clipboard. "Uh… We had a squad shortage. Sharpe's squad is in the shop, so I gave her yours."

"You… Jesus… fuck." I turn away from him, growling. I take my radio out as he breathes a relieved sigh. "Squad thirty-two."

"Go for thirty-two!" Lyric says far too chipper.

"Back to the garage. Now."

"Um… Okay… But it will be a few minutes. I'm a block away, but I'm on a traffic stop."

"Now, Sharpe!" I command.

"Okay! Geez. You don't have to yell." I can hear the pout in her voice. I feel a little bad for yelling at her, but I want my damn squad.

"I don't know why you're commanding her back here. There are no other squads for her to use," Sergeant Jackson says to me.

I look around the garage incredulously. "There are seven squads in this garage. Are you going to sit there and tell me that not a single one of them works? That they all need repairs?"

"Yeah. That's exactly what I'm telling you. One more thing I've been harping about for years. We need the budget to fix them. Instead, they created a fucking taskforce we don't need."

I fold my arms over my chest and shoot a withering glare at him. He has the decency to cower. "So what the fuck were you going to put Mariah in?"

He nods to the one closest to the door. "Check engine light comes on, but we've been advised it's just a sensor."

I'm about to lay into him, but Lyric drives into the garage. Instead, I walk to the passenger side and open the door. "Don't even think about putting her in that squad, Jackson. Double her up with someone or give her Rens' squad."

"I can't fucking double her up! I don't have enough people as it is!" he barks.

"Then put her in Rens' squad! That's a fucking order!" I duck into the passenger side of the unmarked SUV and slam the door.

"What was that about?" Lyric asks quietly.

"Squads. He gave you mine and was going to put Mariah in one that has a check engine light on. Something about it just being a sensor, but I doubt it very seriously." I force my gaze to soften before I look over at her. "Not a fucking chance I'm putting her in a squad that could have a problem. So, I told him to put her in Captain Rens' squad."

"Oh... Okay. Good." She bites her lip as she backs out of the garage. When she hits the streets, she's damn near chewing it.

I force my hands to stay on my thighs like a good boy. "Stop chewing on your lip."

She glances at me, but doesn't stop. "Will he listen?"

I nod. "Yes. Because if he doesn't, he'll meet a suspension and a write-up for being insubordinate. Sort of like you are. Stop chewing your lip."

She ignores me as she drives. Very unprofessional thoughts start flooding my mind. Things like reaching over and running my thumb over her beautiful mouth to stop her from chewing on her lip. Kissing her senseless. Then spanking her ass for ignoring the command. I take a breath and force my gaze out the passenger side window.

"Is Mariah okay? She was... um..." She keeps chewing her lip. "She was upset this morning."

I release a breath and grip my jeans as I look over at her. "She'll be okay. She's better now than she was." I watch as she nods slowly. I know she's probably thinking of all the ways I could have made Mariah feel better. "Lyric. Stop. Chewing. On. Your. Lip."

She lets out an exasperated sigh and shoots a glare at me. "I can chew my damn lip if I want to. I'm upset. I'm upset for her because I know she's sad and upset. Okay? Back the fuck off."

I let out a low growl and narrow my eyes. She jumps slightly and lowers hers. Though she's still glaring. Even pissed off, the girl is gorgeous. Her dark hair is up in a messy bun. Her hazel eyes are burning as she glares. She focuses herself to look back at the road, but I know she's angry because her cheeks flush. Her small, taut body is vibrating as she grips the steering wheel. The knuckles on her small hands turn white.

Lyric is a lot like Mariah in the looks department. Her hair is shorter, but she's close to the same height. She's just as small, though. And her tits are the source of her self-confidence issues. At least they're a large part of it. Like Mariah, they're large. And like Mariah, she wears an Under Armour t-shirt underneath her uniform to hide her cleavage. Even with the bulletproof vest, she has just as much of an issue as Mariah does with hiding them.

Her face is twisted in what I'm sure she thinks is resting bitch face or something. It only succeeds in making me want to throw her against the hood of the squad and fuck her into submission.

"I don't know why she'd talk to you anyway. You're part of the problem. You're part of everyone's problem."

I raise an eyebrow. "Same reason you run straight to DJ. I know how to make her forget."

She lets out a snort of a laugh. "But she doesn't, does she? She still has feelings for three people. Just like I do. Even though one of them is an asshole."

Just like Mariah's admission this morning, hers is like a kick directly to my dick. And just like I had with Mariah, I suck in a breath. Only I'm far more quiet about it with her. Mostly because I'm irritated and pissed off.

I take a breath. "You want to know why Mariah came to me? It's because you have a tendency to do nothing to help her realize that what happened with the two of you isn't a fucking bad thing."

She glances at me. I can see the surprise flicker across her face, but I know she won't say anything about it. "And you want to know why I go to DJ? It's because DJ actually cares about what I have to say."

I chuckle. "You're so fucking stubborn. I know how you feel about him. I know how you feel about Mariah. And just fifteen seconds ago, I figured out how you feel about me. Not so bad for a stupid Lieutenant, huh?"

The words cause her to glare more viciously at the traffic and grip the steering wheel harder. "I didn't call you a stupid Lieutenant the other day. I called you an asshole Lieutenant and said you're too stupid to realize the good thing you have standing in front of you. I was talking about Mariah."

I tear my eyes away from her blushing cheeks. I know now that she also means her, and I hate myself a little bit for it. So, I decide to give her a break. "The reason I said to stop biting your lip, Lyric, is because you're making it fucking bleed." I open the window and rest my elbow on the open frame. I lean my head against my hand and let the air hit my face.

"Oh… I… I'm sorry. I didn't notice," she says quietly. She discreetly licks her lip before putting a shaky thumb to it.

I dare to look at her. She's relaxed, but she's frowning. Almost like she hates herself for mouthing off to me when I was trying to help her. One more thing to add to the list of reasons to like her. She's remorseful when she realizes she fucked up and thinks of ways to fix it. I know that right now she's running over a thousand ways to make it up to me because she thinks she disappointed me.

She may do all she can to keep me at a distance, but I've spent four years around her in some form or other. My relationship with her isn't like it is with Mariah, but I know her. I know her tells. Which is how I know that right now she's deep in thought. And in a few minutes she'll apologize profusely and try to explain it away. Then, she'll do something to try and make me laugh.

I take a chance and reach over to tuck a piece of hair behind her ear. "I know, Lyric."

She smiles, and leans into my hand. The move is so unlike how she usually reacts to me that I leave my hand resting against her cheek. I have to keep my hand from shaking because of the fact that she's showing me a little part of how she really feels beyond just saying the words.

I'd love to hear more, but she doesn't get a chance to say anything before the radio in the squad is going off. I glance at it and slowly remove my hand as she tilts her head. It sounded like DJ's voice, but it was garbled. Almost like someone else was talking over him or something.

Lyric reaches for the mic. "Was that for squad thirty-two?"

"Squad four to squad thirty-two," DJ says again.

"Go ahead," Lyric answers. She looks at me a little fearfully. It's not often DJ calls anyone over the radio. Unless he's on patrol or something. I know he isn't today. After last night, he's decided to hole up in his office.

"I need you and Chance to meet me at Schools Public Warehouse. Bus driver is our contact. He's waiting for us at the main building for the Village Crossing Apartments. Pink building," DJ answers.

"10-4," she says softly

I look at Lyric. "Well, here goes nothing."

She smiles and laughs. "Mariah isn't going to be happy about this. I think she just wanted a quiet day of calls."

I crack up. "Like that would ever fucking happen."

Lyric does a U-turn and heads for the warehouse. I smile because I think this is just the type of call I need today. Something to get my mind right. Anything to stop myself from thinking of the words Mariah and Lyric said about having feelings for three people. I'm happy as hell that I'm one of them, but I feel exactly the same way. Just as confused.

I have feelings for three people and no fucking idea how to deal with them.

Chapter Four

☆ Mariah ☆

I step out of the shower in the locker room with a towel wrapped around me. I've already taken one today, but for some reason, this time it felt amazing. Tension felt like it seeped out of my pores. Odd, considering I hate showers. I don't do well with them at all. I prefer baths.

I walk to my locker, smiling softly. I would be a fool to not admit that it had more to do with Matt than it did with the shower. I've been in love with him since his intense brown eyes first landed on mine.

But I was scared beyond reason. I didn't come here from a happy situation. I hated my life. I was depressed. My anxiety was out of control. So, I decided one day to do the scariest thing I've ever done in my life. File divorce papers and start my own life.

I didn't look back. I showed up in Gainesville with no real reason for moving here except it was in Florida and seemed like a nice place to live. I decided to put my unused degrees to good use and get a job in the one profession I truly wasn't sure if I loved or not.

Law Enforcement.

I never had the chance to explore it. My family hated my decision. Eventually, I just gave in. No one ever really believed I could do it anyway. I had no support. And the little that I did had been taken away by my ex who hated the idea that I spoke to anyone other than him. I lost friends. I lost my family. I lost everything.

All the while, I'd been fighting who I am. When I was in middle school, I'd started to take an interest in boys. I was a little late to the party. A lot of my friends already had boyfriends. Not me. I was too busy focusing on school and being the best.

But there was one boy that I had taken interest in. He was nice to me. He wasn't like the rest. He didn't stare at the double D's I was already sporting by the time I hit eighth grade. He listened to me when I talked and kept his eyes on mine instead of my chest. I thought he was great.

But I'd also started to take notice of the girls in the locker room. Well, mostly just one. She was also my friend. Mostly, I was interested in the fact that all the girls seemed to hide in the bathroom stalls or showers when they got dressed. I thought something was wrong with me because I just wrapped a towel around myself and got dressed. If someone saw my tits when I pulled my bra down and removed the towel, it didn't bother me. It didn't bother my friend either. She did the same thing.

I felt like I was defective in that I never bothered with make-up. I didn't care about designer jeans and tight fitting tank tops. I just wore what I felt comfortable in. I didn't spend hours on my hair. I didn't worry about blow drying it after we were in the pool during gym class.

But what I hated about myself the most was that, though I never gave myself up, I snuck glances at my friend.. I would take quick peeks at her when she was around me while she was applying make-up or doing her hair. Or pulling her jeans up or shirt down.

I thought maybe I was just comparing myself to her. And maybe I was in some ways. It wasn't until high school I got my first real crush, at least that's what I called it, on a girl.Another friend. She was in my history class and sat in front of me. When we first became friends, it was because she had turned around and asked me if I had a pen. I smiled and gave her my extra one. Then spent the entire class wishing I smelled like her, had her hair and body, and looked as good as she did wearing white.

I went home that night and cried so hard I ended up sick. The reason? Because I couldn't get the image of her cleavage out of my head. I kept thinking of touching her. Which made me touch myself. I'd never done that up until that point.

I'd always been told to keep my hands above the blankets. Touching myself was wrong. Sex before marriage was wrong. Self-satisfaction was not important as long as my significant other was happy. And it was also wrong.

Which is why when I got to the point where my stomach clenched and my clit started feeling a delicious tingle, I stopped. I didn't know what was happening. I'd never felt that before, but I knew it was wrong. It was dirty. And it was happening with thoughts of a girl. Someone I had lunch with that day. Someone I would go on to having lunch with every single day after. It had never happened with a guy. It made me cry even more.

I understood a long time ago that I was different. I was attracted to both males and females. But the older I got, the more I repressed it because I didn't feel like it was right. Ironically, though, I have a cousin who is gay. But I saw how my father reacted to him. I never had any issues with him or his lifestyle. I'd always admired that he was able to live his life how he chose to. I never saw anything wrong with it.

But I'd always thought something was wrong with *me*. Even though I've always advocated for true love, no matter the sex of the partner. Part of me knew it didn't make sense. How could I be so supportive of my cousin and his choice to love another man, but think that I was a bad person? Even I knew how fucked up it was to think that way.

I did very well in keeping everyone in the dark about who I truly was. Who I am. I got married. I did what everyone thought I should do. I lived my life how everyone thought I should. I put my life and dreams and aspirations aside and took care of my husband. I ignored my needs. I put him above everything else. Including my well-being and mental health. Like a good little girl.

I wipe my eyes as I start to get dressed. When I moved here, I started to learn to discover myself. Lyric and I became fast friends. We were in the same training class. We moved in together before training was through. I never told her that I was attracted to her. She never said it to me either, but she'd always been very open with me. I know she's pansexual. She's attracted to people for who they are. It was all very scary to me.

I had also formed a very close relationship with Matt almost right away. He's not well-liked. He's surly. He has an attitude and a reputation for being hard. People openly call him an asshole. But he'd never been like that with me. I was one of the few who got to see who he truly is. I love it. I've loved him since he first opened his mouth.

I hated that he friend-zoned me long ago. Instead of taking me out to dinner, Matt invited me to his house to watch the games. To him, I've always just been one of the guys. I have a lot in common with him. I'm easy to talk to. For him, that's all it's really been.

The first time I got truly drunk with Lyric was because of Matt. I wanted more with him. I'd never felt the things I felt for him for anyone else. I had sort of tried to broach the subject. I asked him if he wanted to go to dinner at a restaurant I wanted to try. It had been almost two years. Two years of him teasing me about getting in my pants. I knew he was kidding because he'd always made it clear that he was.

But that night I found myself too wasted and upset with him after he told me that he was busy that night. He'd planned something with DJ and some girl. It was then I decided I hated DJ and Matt and was done with men. Why not give into the other side of me? Lyric would never hurt me like that.

After it was done, I cried so hard I threw up. I didn't sleep at all that night. I thought I should feel dirty. But I didn't. It felt right. I was terrified and didn't know why. My mind raced. I called myself every name in the book. Including a dirty whore.

The next day, though I wasn't working, I went into the office. I went directly to Matt because despite the fact that I was upset with him, I realized that he was the only one I could turn to. When I was through spilling my guts, I begged Matt to make good on his teasing. I needed to feel normal. Normal to me was a woman and man.

I'd never had an orgasm before Lyric. No one, including myself, had ever made me come. I didn't know where to touch. My ex didn't care about my needs, sexual or otherwise. The one other person I was with tried. It's something I'll always love him for, but he also never succeeded. It was one more thing that made me feel defective. Not normal. How could the only person to make me come be a woman? It was just like high school all over again when the only time I'd ever been close was to thoughts of a woman.

I finish getting dressed and start putting on my gear. I check my gun and put it in its holster. I check my taser and put it away as well. I make sure my cuffs are secured in their pouch and my flashlight is properly strapped onto my belt. I check my retractable baton and put it in its pouch. I make sure I have my extra magazines for my gun.

I take a breath and start putting up my hair. Matt didn't disappoint. And he hasn't since. Matt has both held me while I cried and rocked my world when I needed him to. It's made me fall so much more in love with him than I already had been. But I knew he didn't want more. Matt is happy with his life. He likes being able to come and go as he pleases and mess around with whoever he wants to.

It's the reason I haven't allowed anything other than his fingers or his tongue in me. Despite the fact that my body, mind, and heart scream at me every time to let him take it all the way. Instead, I satiate the need by giving him a blowjob that makes him see stars. I feel like it's the least I can do for him as a thank you for all he does for me.

I chuckle to myself at the thought. It really is stupid when I think back. I'm so ridiculously in love with Matt that I'll take whatever I can get from him, even though it will never be enough, just so I can get thoughts of the man and woman I've been in love with for just as long as him out of my head.

I wipe the frustrated tears from my eyes as I turn on my radio. I know as soon as I walk out to the garage Sergeant Jackson is going to start yelling at me. He's hated me ever since I started here. I still don't know why. I usually don't ask for anything from Matt regarding my job. Favors just because of our relationship doesn't sit well with me. Today, though, I felt it was more than necessary. I needed to get my head right. I hate taking advantage of his position, but I also don't want to lose my job.

"Squad four to squad twelve."

I sigh and slump onto the bench. Of course DJ would have to pick now to jump in. As if I don't have enough on my mind with Matt and Lyric. He has to add himself into the mix just to make my life more chaotic. Though, he is the other man in my life that makes me run directly to Matt so I can forget about him.

"Go ahead," I say softly. I hadn't intended to let the tears be heard in my voice, but it cracks. I know DJ heard it. Everyone did.

"You didn't respond when I said we have a case. I didn't know if you heard."

I take a breath and close my eyes. "No... I... I'm just coming on now."

"Are you still at HQ?"

I nod and then remember that he can't see me. "10-4."

"Well, meet me in the garage."

I nod again and sniffle as I open my eyes. "Okay."

My voice cracks again. I hate myself for it. I hate showing weakness to those I'm close to. Showing it to everyone is torture. Even though the rest of the officers on duty today can't see me, I know they can hear me. I hate that they can hear the weaknesses I'm trying so hard to fight.

I swore when I moved here that no one would ever make me feel weak or small or worthless again. I promised myself I'd be strong. I'd be fearless. I would only show vulnerabilities in the privacy of my own home. So far, I don't think I've kept any of my promises to myself.

I shake my head as I walk to the garage. Sergeant Jackson is sitting on a chair near the garage door entrance reading a paper. He's wearing a scowl. I already know I'm going to face his wrath for all of the staffing shortages we have. It's one of many things he enjoys taking out on me. What I don't understand is why he's still here. He should be out on patrol. Matt went out there for me so I wouldn't have to deal with him.

"It's about fucking time," he growls without looking at me.

I flinch at the snarl. "Sorry, sir."

He points to a squad by the door. "That's yours today. Get your ass out there. I have shit to do. I don't have time to wait around all day for your pretty little ass to decide to come to work."

I blink at his tone. He's being more of an asshole than usual. I take a breath. "I'm meeting Captain Rens. We -"

"I said get going, Carter!" he yells as he looks up at me. "I don't give a shit who you're meeting! Staff is short! You aren't helping! Get your ass in that squad and -"

"Hey!" DJ's deep voice barks from behind me.

I wrap my arms around myself like I'm hugging myself. I look down at the ground and blink back the tears. I'm trying not to tremble, but Jackson has never been quite this snappy with me. He's never actually screamed at me.

"Captain!" Sergeant Jackson has the decency to at least sound afraid. But I don't dare look up. I'm not in control yet.

DJ stops behind me. He puts his hand on my lower back and almost instantly calms me. "Please tell me I did not just hear a Sergeant who has been with this department for almost fifteen years screaming at an officer like that." DJ's voice is deadly.

"I... we... I need her -"

"On the streets. Yeah. I got that. The whole fucking department got that. I also noticed that for some fucking reason, you don't have a radio on you. Which baffles me because I swear I heard your voice barking at Lieutenant Chance not too long ago. Or am I just getting old and senile?"

"Sir, it's -"

"Not on your person. Or on, for that matter. If it were, you'd have heard Officer Carter has been called out."

I bite my lip, still refusing to look up. I can hear Sergeant Jackson huffing and puffing. The venom that drips from DJ's commanding voice should strike fear into me. It definitely does in Sergeant Jackson. To me, though, it helps to center me. I've never understood it. His voice to me has the same effect that Matt's hugs do.

DJ says nothing more. I can feel Sergeant Jackson's glare on my back as DJ steers us to his unmarked squad.

I clear my throat. "He wants me in the squad by the door," I nearly whisper. "I can meet you wherever you want me to."

DJ opens the passenger side door to his squad and waits for me to get it. "Mariah, every squad in here needs to be fixed. I'm not putting you in that squad. The check engine light is on. I just got the order for it on my desk this morning. They think it's a sensor, but it dies out. Probably spark plugs, but you could get stranded somewhere."

I suck in a breath as he closes the door gently when he steps back. I look at Sergeant Jackson. I can feel myself start trembling. DJ opens the driver's side door. "Did he know?"

DJ closes his door after he sits down. "Yes. He has a clipboard that has all the available squads that can be used. Every squad in here has a problem. Except mine and the commanding officers. He was under orders to put you in my squad today and Lyric in Matt's." He glances at me as he pulls out of the garage. "I know you're pissed at me, Rih, but I care about you. I'm always going to protect you. Keep you safe."

I put up a hand to stop him from talking and look out the window. I take a shuddering breath and reach up to wipe the stray tear that fell.

"I…" I shake my head and close my eyes as I put my hand down. "I'm not pissed at you," I whisper.

He chuckles. "Could have fooled me."

I nod. "It's me. I'm pissed at me. I… have a lot… on my mind."

I feel him hesitantly take my hand. He gives it a gentle squeeze as he drives. "You know you can talk to me," he says quietly.

I try to keep the tremble out of my hand, but fail. He squeezes it again. I open my eyes and look down at my lap. "It's hard… to talk about. I don't understand it myself."

He's quiet for a few moments before he takes a breath. "Does it have to do with Matt?"

I don't look up at him. "Sort of. It's just… It's so… complicated. Scary. I don't understand it."

He rubs his thumb in small circles over the back of my hand. "I know I'm not as close to you as Matt is. I know what I said hurt you. I know you'd probably talk to Lyric or Matt over me, but I'm always here for you. Okay?"

I glance at him. DJ added into the mix of my mess of a life only complicates everything more. The other day when he'd made a comment about how I'd look sprawled on his desk sent every feeling I have for him straight to my clit. I haven't told him how I feel about him, or how I've felt it for just as long as I have for Lyric and Matt.

I have been starting to explore them, though. I feel so guilty for feeling the way I do, but I have started to understand that I need to try and make sense of everything. Sort it out. I can't do that if I sit in a corner and hide from them.

Trying to explore them was the reason I ended up with my tongue buried in Lyric's pussy last night. I hadn't expected myself to feel so wrong and guilty about it. I convinced myself before I did it that it was okay. I kept hearing Matt's words running through my head. Today isn't the first time he's told me I'm pansexual. It's not the first time he's said it's okay. I know about his feelings for Lyric. I also know how he feels about DJ. Matt wears his heart on his sleeve. Much like me.

It's probably why we get along. Why I'm so hopeless for him.

I shake the thoughts from my head. Sorting out my feelings for three people will have to wait. Right now, we have an issue our taskforce has been assigned.

DJ pulls into the lot of the Village Apartments main building. He lets go of my hand and gives me a soft and surprisingly supportive smile. "Ready?"

"Ready." I smile gratefully back at him. I don't know if he knows how much he's calmed me. Just being around him makes me calmer. We both get out of the squad. My eyes fall to Lyric and Matt casually leaning against the hood of Matt's squad.

"I mean, if you're asking, I'm sure I can make it look innocent." Matt smirks at her.

Lyric laughs and shoots him an incredulous look. "This is a busy street, Lieutenant. Not a chance in hell."

He winks. "Then quit shooting that pretty little mouth off, or we'll be testing the suspension of the squad."

Lyric squeaks. "Oh my God, you're impossible."

"Sexy."

"Impossible."

Matt shrugs and throws her a cocky smile. "You can't say you don't wonder."

Lyric's eyes widen as she looks up at him. "Asshole. Impossible, and an asshole." She stomps her foot so adorably that I laugh.

"Makes me wonder what we missed," DJ says low enough for only me to hear. His breath against my ear makes me shiver.

"I promise. I'm good at what I do." Matt nods towards me. "Ask Mariah."

My mouth drops. "Matt!"

He laughs. "I'm teasing her, honey."

Lyric gives me a wicked smile that makes me quiver. She looks up at Matt. "You know what? Let's go for it. See just how good that suspension is." She makes a move to open the back door.

Matt's eyes darken, but he hauls her away from the door. He slaps her ass. I jump for her. "Work to do, brat."

She giggles and winks at DJ and I when she walks by us. "He wasn't saying that a minute ago."

"Fuck me," DJ growls. I don't think he thinks anyone else hears him, but I do.

Matt leans down and whispers in my ear as he passes by us. "Put in a good word for me, huh?"

I elbow him lightly. "You're fucking awful."

"Alright. Enough fucking around. We do actually have a job to do," DJ says. I feel his hand on my belt. He pulls me back to him. Lyric and Matt sit on the bumper bars of DJ's squad as DJ hides behind me. I glance back at him. "Don't," he whispers. "Just stay there a minute."

I bite my lip to keep from giggling when I feel his hand brush my ass. I know he's adjusting himself. I don't know why I find that adorable, or why it sends tingles all through me. For the first time, I just allow myself to feel.

And what I feel is a little lighter at the thought that I just may get through this. I know we all have some type of feelings for each other. Maybe my skills of working things out can be put to use here.

Chapter Five

☆ DJ ☆

I peel the label off my bottle of beer with a soft smile on my face. We spoke with our contact regarding the drug trafficking and were able to take out a few key players who didn't know we were coming.

We were lucky. We didn't have the time to set up a proper takedown. Instead, we called in our SWAT team and took the suspects down as swiftly and cleanly as possible. After our interviews with those we arrested, we ended up with a lot of information and were able to set up surveillance on the gang responsible. All in all, it was a good day.

Which is why I hate the fact that my mood isn't as high as the others at my table. Even Mariah seems to be smiling and happy. Considering how angsty she was today, it's surprising. Though, it's very nice to see her beautiful face light up.

The music blaring through the speakers in the bar is like nails on a chalkboard to my ears. I picked karaoke night of all nights to make my move on the three people in front of me. After my night with Matt last night, I wanted to just say fuck it. Forget it.

But even I knew the statement was idiotic. I didn't want to forget it. I really didn't think that he did either. Still, the words rolled off my

46

tongue. I said we should forget it happened. We should keep going on as things were.

At the time, I figured it was the best option. I know Matt is pretty torn between Mariah and Lyric. I'm torn between them just as much. Adding him into my fucked up life makes it all worse. Fuck if I don't want it, though. I want them all.

Which is why the words I'm about to say are startling. I've had most of the day to think about them and what I want. The truth is, I want all three of them. I can't imagine my life without them in it. I don't want to forget about anything that's happened between any of us.

"I think we all need to talk about where we all stand," I blurt. I look up as Matt and Lyric stop talking. The noise of the bar is kind of loud, but I don't have to talk real loud to be heard.

"Nope," Lyric shakes her head after a moment. She stands. "Not drunk enough for this." She takes her drink and heads directly for the bar.

I chuckle and turn towards a silent Mariah. Only she's not at my side where she had been. "Uh…" I look up at Matt. "Where the fuck did Mariah go?"

He watches me and leans back in his chair. He takes a drink of his beer. He puts it down on the table slowly. "She turned invisible right when you said that. Probably halfway to Colorado by now." He leans forward again and looks down at his bottle. "Where the hell did that come from?"

"Look. Matt, I know what I said earlier. It was a stupid as fuck thing to say. But -"

"I don't want to forget it."

I sigh. "Fuck. Thank God," I say quietly.

"I've been thinking all day on how to move on with all of this. We all like each other. We need to figure it out. I don't know how, but it needs to happen because we're all fucking miserable."

"I just can't handle this shit anymore." I shake my head. "We've all been together in some way long enough. You and Mariah. Me and Lyric. Us." I nod towards Lyric as she downs four shots then turns with refills on our drinks for all of us. "Them."

Matt chuckles. "How are we going to play this, Cap?"

I run a hand down my face. "I don't know, man. It's why we need to talk about it. I'm not willing to walk away from any of you. We've been dancing around each other too long."

47

"Agreed."

Lyric sits down next to Matt with a hesitant smile. "Can we maybe loosen up a little more? I can't have this conversation right now. There's still a lot I don't understand."

Matt chuckles as he pops the top off his next bottle. "Bottoms up." He puts an arm around the back of her chair. She giggles.

I can't help but laugh as I start drinking my own. "Seriously. These singers shouldn't be allowed up there. They're really bad."

"I know. This was a bad night to decide to show up here," Matt says.

"There have been few good ones. That country singer that sang that Reba McEntire song was really good." Lyric sips her drink.

"Yeah. I guess that's true. There was another guy who sang a Jason Aldean song I liked," I say. I start to loosen up, feeling better about the upcoming conversation. I'm tired of the run-around we've all been doing with each other. It's time to just be upfront and honest.

Lyric leans into Matt and drops her hand on his thigh. Her legs are crossed, but I can feel her foot against my leg. Lyric's touch always manages to make my blood boil. Now is no exception. I glance around for Mariah again as I get up.

"Can you get Mariah another sex on the beach?" Lyric asks, looking up at me through her lashes.

I chuckle and lean down. "Anything you want," I whisper. I trail my hand up her thigh and give her pussy a gentle squeeze as I head for the bar. Nothing I haven't done before. Lyric is very open with me.

She trembles under my touch just like she always does. "Not fair."

"Oh, we don't play fair, honey," Matt rumbles. I chuckle as a shiver finds its way down my spine. Matt's voice is deep with a hint of a Southern accent. Not the deep South like mine, but enough that anyone would be wishing for his breath on their neck.

It makes me go spiraling directly back to last night when he had me pinned against the couch. I groan quietly and shake my head as the bartender hands me my drinks. I bring them back to the table and pull my chair closer to Lyric.

"Really. Where is Mariah?" I ask, putting the drinks on the table.

"She wasn't really feeling well," Matt says.

I take a last look around the bar, getting a little worried, but I settle in and pop the top off my bottle. I look over at Matt and Lyric. My eyes widen. I glance under the table, then back at Lyric. She's gripping Matt's thigh. She's turned into his shoulder and gripping his shirt with her other hand. Matt is casually glancing around the bar. His arm is slung over the back of her chair. But his other hand is between her legs.

My mouth drops. "Are you fingering her right now?" I whisper as I pull my chair closer to shield her. The effort is fruitless. No one is looking at us, but it's my way of protecting both of them.

Matt smiles and winks. "It's her fault. She said she was all wet and needed to clean up. I couldn't let her relieve the pressure herself."

"Fuck, Matt," I groan for no other reason than because I know how Lyric feels and am fighting myself from joining in. We all have to be fucking drunk to even entertain anything that's happening right now.

Lyric whimpers into his shoulder and clears her throat as she shudders. "Matt. God…," she whispers. I know she's coming.

He slowly pulls his fingers out of her and adjusts her panties. "Not God. But close."

She swats him lightly as he casually sucks her off his fingers like it's something he does every day. I groan again and give into my need to touch her. I drop my hand on her thigh and squeeze it lightly.

"Makes me wonder how many times you've done that in a fucking bar." I grin and take a sip of my beer.

"You don't want me to answer that." He takes a look around the bar. "Okay. For real. Where is Mariah?"

"I'm starting to think she had an anxiety attack," I say. "She's been on edge all day."

Lyric's eyes shoot to mine. "She hasn't had one in over a year."

"I know, honey," I say. "But she disappeared. It's been quite a while now." I look at my watch. "Twenty minutes."

"I'm going to check on her." Lyric starts to get up, but pauses. "Oh… my… God." Her eyes fixate on the stage behind me.

"What?" I start to turn.

"Oh, shit," Matt says.

My mouth drops when I see her. "Shit. Is she actually going to sing? I thought she never sang in front of anyone."

"She only sings in front of people she trusts," Lyric says softly. "Unless she's trying to be brave... She used to do karaoke all the time. She won a contest once."

I watch as Mariah takes the mic from the DJ. "Trying to be brave?" I ask.

Matt clears his throat. "She's fighting panic. She's refusing to succumb to it. Singing is her way to calm down."

I turn my chair so I can look at the stage without straining. I drop my hand on Lyric's thigh once more. Matt puts his arm over the back of both our chairs and rests his hand against my back. Lyric leans against me as Matt leans against her. I smile because it feels fucking right. Almost. Only one person is missing.

Mariah pushes her hair behind her ear with a soft smile that makes her even more beautiful. Her sun-kissed skin almost sparkles under the stage lights. She takes her place in the center of it, holding the mic protectively in front of her with one hand. The other is wrapped tightly around her waist. To anyone else, she might seem like she belongs up there. To the three of us, we can see her struggle.

But it doesn't stop the girl from showcasing her inner strength. I've seen people with anxiety. A lot of them are the strongest people I know. Some allow themselves to succumb to it. Unfortunately, in my line of work, I've seen those who haven't made it.

Not this girl. She's too fucking tenacious to allow it to rule her life. So, even though her breathing quickens when more and more curious eyes start to fall on her because of the sudden cut in music, she's standing there like a soldier. Like some kind of unyielding force of nature ready to destroy all that stands in her way. In this case, the anxiety that makes her feel weak.

I've only ever seen one other person in this world fight it like Mariah does. And that girl is sitting right next to me. Everyday, she wakes up and throws on her big girl panties. Sometimes, they don't quite fit, and she ends up in my office. And it's those days that I watch my girl turn into my own superhero. She might take a few minutes, but after she paces it out and talks a little to herself, she throws on her cape and hits the streets, ready to save the city from itself.

It's one of the most beautiful things I've ever seen.

"For the first time ever in our quaint little establishment is Mariah. She'll be singing us a little Mariah Carey. Not often we see anyone try to take on the legend, but I've been assured we'll be blown away." The DJ winks as he starts the music. A beautiful melody starts before Mariah starts singing.

"Doesn't it ever stay? Must it always fade away? Couldn't love ever be something tangible and real? Farewell, fair weather friend. Abandonment returns to taunt me again."

Mariah's voice cracks slightly, but I can't tell if it's because she's scared or crying. I let my hand fall from Lyric's thigh as I lean forward.

Mariah takes a breath and looks directly at Matt. *"I only wanted you to stay. Linger and mean the words you said. Foolishly, I romanticized someone was saving my life for the first time. I only wanted you to be there when I opened up my eyes."*

"Holy… Christ…," Matt whispers.

Mariah lowers her eyes a moment before looking back up at Lyric. *"I was caught in your masquerade. Wish I'd stayed beneath my veil. But it just seemed so easy to open up myself to you. Once more into the wind the embers scatter, and the chill settles in."*

Lyric sniffles. "Oh my God… I think…"

I can only nod. "She saw, and it hurt."

"Saw what?" Matt asks, confused.

"Us," Lyric whispers.

I can hear the tears in Mariah's voice as she sings. She doesn't look at any of us. Instead, she closes her eyes as her voice hits every single note with more emotion than I know what to do with. *"I only wanted you to stay. Linger and mean the words you said. Foolishly, I romanticized someone was saving my life for the first time. I only wanted you to be there when I opened up my eyes."*

"Fuck…," I whisper to myself as I choke up. I wipe away a tear as I take a drink to try and hide it.

Mariah opens her eyes. I know what's coming before she even does it. Her eyes fall on mine. My eyes tear up even more when I see the ones she tries to hide falling from hers. *"Oh, I only wanted you to stay. Linger and mean the words you said."* Her voice starts to soar the more feeling she throws into the song. *"Foolishly, I romanticized someone was saving my life for the first time. I only wanted you to be the one to get me through the night."*

"I... didn't..." Matt takes a deep breath.

Mariah wipes away another tear. "*I only wanted you to be there when I opened up my eyes. Oh, doesn't it ever stay? I only wanted you to stay.*"

As the music fades out, there isn't a single sound. No one is talking. I doubt anyone is breathing. All eyes are riveted to her and her performance. Out of the corner of my eye, I can see a few people glancing towards our table. It was obvious to everyone who she was singing for. And we all deserved it. All of it.

The DJ clears his throat and obviously wipes away his own tear. "Uh... Ladies. Gentleman. That was, um... Mariah. Give her a hand."

The bar erupts in applause, but Mariah's eyes haven't left us. She's broken. I can see it. I watch as she hands the DJ the mic and quickly leaves the stage. She drops her head. Her beautiful, long dark locks fall in front of her eyes. She doesn't bother to push it back. She refuses to look up. Instead of coming back to the table, Mariah moves directly for the door.

"I'll go after her," Lyric whispers, jumping down from the chair.

Matt gently takes her arm. "No. That was my fault. I'll go."

I shake my head at both of them and get up. "No. I should be the one."

I don't give them time to argue or react. I follow Mariah outside. It's dark. The lot really isn't that well-lit. I don't see Mariah initially.

But I can hear her.

What I hear breaks me in pieces.

I follow the sound of her gut-wrenching sobs. She's on her knees in the dirt of the parking lot next to her car. She's rocking back and forth and hugging herself as tightly as she can. Considering she's wearing a pair of very short jean cut-offs, and her legs are completely bare, I know it has to hurt. The rocks must be digging into her skin.

I kneel down at her side facing her. "Rih," I say just above a whisper. I reach out and gently grip her shoulder.

She jerks away just as I anticipated. "Just l-leave, DJ... I c-can't... I can't." She cries harder when she tries to take a deep breath.

I've seen panic attacks before. I know she's crying partly because she saw us with Lyric, and partly because she's panicking and can't calm down. I reach out again and tenderly push her hair out of her face. "Mariah. Take a breath, honey." I keep my voice steady because I know it's what she needs, but it's not the easiest thing I've ever done.

"Just g-go." She pushes herself against the car as closely as she can, and as far from me as she can get.

"No, honey. I'm not leaving you in this state." I gently rub her back and take a step forward so I'm closer to her. "Mariah, I'm sorry. I'm sorry for what you saw in there." I take her hand in mine and slowly stand. "I don't want to talk about this out here, baby. Come to my car. Or we can stay here, and get in yours. Just not out here."

She shivers and shakes her head. "My k-keys." She hiccups. "I d-dropped them."

I drop to my hands and knees to look under the car. I easily reach them, but she would have had to lay in the dirt. Her arms aren't long enough. I take her keys and her hand. I pull her up slowly with me. I help her into her car and quickly stride to the passenger side. Mariah wipes at her eyes as she breathes deeply.

I lean over and hug her because I know her well enough to know she needs it. "I'm sorry, honey," I whisper against her neck. "I said that I wanted to talk about where things stood with us. Lyric went to get more drinks. I looked over and you were gone."

"I went to the… bathroom." She doesn't put her arms around me, but I feel her hand grip the hem of my shirt. "I didn't hear you say… that. I must have… gone before."

"Lyric came back with drinks. I had intended to say we all like each other. We need to figure out this thing that's going on. Because it's not helping us. It's doing nothing but hurting us all. But I wanted to wait until you'd gotten back." I tangle my fingers in her hair. She slowly begins to stop trembling.

"I had a stomachache. It took a… little longer," she whispers.

I nod into her neck and give into kissing her shoulder. I keep my lips against her skin. "You still weren't back when I went to get another round. We'd all drank the one Lyric got pretty quickly because of the conversation we were about to have. I think we were all feeling pretty loosened up after that. We all started feeling a little flirty."

She sniffles. "I'd say."

I kiss her neck and hug her tighter. I can feel her pulse jumping. "When I got back, Matt was helping Lyric out with the… situation she found herself in. I touched her and made her wet. It's nothing I haven't done before. I wasn't expecting to come back to Matt relieving the pressure. It shocked me, but… Well, I wasn't going to stop it. I know how much they've been circling around each other. Like a couple of other people I know." I smile against her neck. "Maybe I should have put a stop to it until we'd talked."

Mariah shakes her head and slowly pulls away. She wipes her eyes. "I shouldn't have gotten upset." She smiles softly, but I can tell it's hard. She turns and traces her steering wheel cover.

I tangle one hand in her hair and drop the other on her thigh. I stay turned towards her. "Mariah, it's okay. You had a reason to be. Talk to me. Tell me."

She takes a breath and shrugs. "I guess… I just felt left out." She looks down at her lap. "I wanted to… talk about things. I wanted to tell you all how I feel. I was trying to work up the courage, but I have a nervous stomach. It got upset on me."

I lightly rub my thumb over her thigh. "I get it."

She bites her lip. "I sort of felt like… I don't know. Lyric is in such a different place than I am. And I truly admire her for it. I wish I were like her. But… I'd never be able to just… let you touch me like that in a bar. Maybe p-privately… But not like that." She shakes her head. "I'm so in awe of her."

I smile and lean over. I kiss her cheek and squeeze her thigh. "Look at me."

She takes a deep breath and looks up at me slowly. "I'm sorry. If that's w-what you want -"

I shake my head. "Ssh…" I kiss the corner of her mouth. "That's not what I want. I want you. I want all of you. But I'd never make you do anything you aren't comfortable with, Mariah." I reach up and wipe a tear away. "We need to talk to them about where we stand, and what we want, but if you want to talk one on one first, I'm okay with that. I know you and I aren't where you are with them. I also know that you aren't exactly comfortable with a lot of things about yourself. So maybe we need to have a conversation ourselves first. Would that make you feel a little less overwhelmed with things?"

She searches my eyes for several moments. "I'd… I'd like that," she finally whispers.

I lean in again and pause. I keep one hand tangled in her hair. The other cups her cheek as I watch her. I could get lost in her blue eyes. She slowly closes them and leans into my hand as she leans forward. She grips my wrist softly as her lips brush mine.

I smile and pull her in the last couple of millimeters. I kiss her gently, letting her set the pace. I'm not at all surprised when I feel the same fireworks I feel with Lyric and Matt also ignite with her. When she presses closer, I deepen the kiss with a low moan.

I let her kiss me for as long as she wants to, but when I feel her start to tremble and grip my jeans dangerously close to my hardening cock, I take her wrist gently. I slowly pull away with a smile. I run my thumb across her lower lip and kiss her softly.

"Let me take you home. We'll come back for your car tomorrow. I'll text Matt and tell him to work it out with the bar, but we need to talk. I don't want to do it in the car."

She nods. "Okay." She smiles shyly and looks at me through her lashes.

"Beautiful," I whisper.

She blushes as we get out of the car. She locks her doors as I text Matt. I take her hand and lead her to my car. I can tell she's nervous by the slight shake of her hand. Mariah feels like she's holding the entire weight of the world on her shoulders.

My job is to lighten her load any way I can.

Chapter Six

☆ Lyric ☆

(Two Weeks Later)

I rub the sleep out of my eyes and yawn as I reach for my phone. The sun isn't up. I don't know what time it is, but I'm not happy about being woken up so early in the damn day.

"What?" I bark into the receiver when I finally manage to answer it. I close my eyes against the LED light. Even though the brightness is turned all the way down, it's still bright as fuck at whatever God awful hour this is.

"How do you feel about picking up a shift?" a gravelly voice asks me.

I look at my caller ID and inwardly groan. "Sergeant Jackson?"

"No. The fucking Easter Bunny. Yes. Sergeant Jackson. I need a couple extra men, but I called them all already. You're the next best thing."

I blink incredulously. "I don't know if I heard that right considering I'm still not totally sure if I'm awake or sleeping, but I think you need a time out. I'll be there." I hang up the phone before he responds.

Normally, I wouldn't pick up an overtime shift because I already work a lot. Add in the taskforce I'm on, and I'm always working it seems. Lucky for Sergeant Asshole, though, I need the extra money because I am working on a surprise. Something I've had in the works for a while. I had almost saved up what I needed to, but now I have two other people to include in the mix.

I smile to myself as I start to get up. Mariah gives me an adorable whimper. It makes me smile more. I lean down and kiss her as I gently untangle myself from her. She mumbles something unintelligible that makes me giggle.

I lean down and nuzzle her. I give her a featherlight kiss. "Sleep, love."

She tries to pull me back. "Warm."

I giggle again. "So are you." I take her hand and kiss her palm.

She groans and blinks sleepily. "Where are you going?"

"They need an extra person today. I thought I'd take the shift."

She sits up slowly. "You hate taking overtime shifts."

"I do, but…" I chew my lip. "I… sort of am working towards something. I have been for a while, but I don't want to tell you what. Don't make me."

She watches me a moment before nodding and slowly getting up. "Okay." She grabs a hoodie and heads for the door of the bedroom. "I'll use the other bathroom. You can get dressed and showered and stuff."

I smile as I watch her walk out of the room. I didn't realize a hoodie and panties could look so sexy. But the first time I saw her wearing them, I instantly decided I was wrong. I'm pretty sure she could make anything look good, but I think when she wears that, it's my favorite.

I head for the shower and step into it after I adjust my spray. I moan at the warm water cascading down my body. Aching bones or sore muscles that I may wake up with are always so much more relaxed after a hot shower.

It's been just about two weeks since the four of us sat down and had our talk. I was more than surprised to hear that everyone felt the exact same way for each other as I did. We'd all been ignoring it because we hated the idea of having feelings for more than one person. Society conditions us to believe that loving more than one person is wrong. My whole life, I believed everyone was right.

Then I met Mariah, DJ, and Matt. I didn't want to admit it, but I was ass over head for all of them rather quickly. Given what I believed, though, I picked one. I picked DJ because he's dominant. He's in control. He appeals to the natural submissive in me, and I loved how he made me feel. I loved how I felt so special with him. At least during the moment. I still do love that about him. I hated how I felt afterwards, but I loved how he makes me feel when I'm with him. Now, I have that feeling I love all of the time. I don't feel bad about being with him. Or about my feelings for any of them.

I knew how DJ felt about Mariah quite a while ago. He'd told me because I caught him watching her one day. He said he felt like an asshole because he knew how much I liked him. I had to convince him that it didn't hurt me. It really didn't because I felt exactly the same way. I even knew that he and Matt had some time together, and that they both liked each other, too.

What was so incredibly difficult for us all is that we were having a hard time admitting that we truly have deep feelings for every person in this little foursome of ours. It was tough because we'd all been conditioned to believe that a relationship like what ours is becoming isn't normal. Maybe it isn't, but it's normal for us. The illusive greatest love of all.

I shut the water off and step out. I dry off and quickly get dressed. I put my hair up and put my gear on. I grab my bag. I sling it over my shoulder and follow my nose to the kitchen. Mariah is swaying to music that must be in her own head. I could watch her all day, but I know I have to get going.

I giggle. "You're very pretty."

She turns her head and blushes. "So are you." She turns off the burner and starts assembling something. "I made you an egg and bacon English muffin. I put the caramel mocha latte in a to-go cup for you." She turns and points to my favorite aluminum to-go cup.

I laugh as she hands me the breakfast sandwich. "It's a crumpet. You Americans are so funny."

She laughs as I take a bite of the sandwich, moaning at the taste. "You're American."

"Maybe now. But I still would never call this an English muffin. It's so -"

"Very English."

I laugh. "Okay. Whatever you say." I smile. "So…, how are you feeling? Now that you've had a couple of weeks to digest everything."

She leans on the counter. "Honestly? I'm still having a bit of a hard time. It's kind of why I've been avoiding everyone and took time off. I think the stress Jackson induces just by opening his mouth topped off with the admission of… well, all of us. I just needed time to really figure things out. But I'm actually coming to terms with who I am." She blushes shyly and looks down at the counter. "I didn't cry or wake up sick after we… you know…"

I smile shyly to myself at the thought of what the two of us did last night. There was no guilt between us for the first time. Neither of us were drunk. It wasn't happening because we were trying to forget about something else that happened that day. It was slow. Passionate. It was like we were making love to each other instead of chasing some kind of release. So beautiful. Thinking about it now has me tingling all over.

I finish my sandwich and reach over to hug her quickly. "I'm sorry. I have to get going. I don't want his wrath."

She winces. "He needs to get laid."

I blink at her, then crack up. "Oh my God, Mariah!"

She smiles brightly. "Something to help you along today."

I kiss her cheek. "Thank you. I'm really proud of you. I hope you know that."

She smiles shyly. "It's all very new. But I really am trying. I think I'm making progress. One step at a time."

I run my fingers through her hair and kiss her softly. "You are."

She nuzzles me. "Go. You're going to be late. Will you say hi to Matt and DJ for me? Tell them I'm getting there? I have talked to them, but I think they're both upset with me because I've only been wanting to spend time with one of them at a time."

I smile softly from the door. "Rih, they aren't. They understand. We're all taking this at the pace we need to."

She looks down. "I'm so far behind you all in my comfort level with everything."

"You also just acknowledged a part of who you are. And it's a part that we've all acknowledged about ourselves and come to terms with a long time ago. It's okay that you're taking things at a different pace then we are. It doesn't mean we feel any differently about you than before." I watch her and smile when I see her smile a little. "You'll get there, Mariah. We all will. It's just like any other relationship. It takes work."

"Wise words."

I shrug and giggle. "Words I've been told by a couple sexy guys a time or two. Or ten."

She laughs. "Have a good day, Lyric."

"You, too!" I close the door behind me and head for my car.

It doesn't take me long to get to the police station. Traffic is slow this early in the morning. It's my favorite time of day. It's so peaceful. The sun hasn't quite woken up, but the sky is just beginning to lighten. There's still stars in the sky. The moon is still visible. Sometimes, if I need to think, I sit on the balcony during this time of day and watch the sun rise into the sky. It's like it gives me clarity.

I look at the time. Almost six in the morning. That gives me a little time before turnout. Enough time to check in with Matt and let him know I'll be out there. It's become a routine. Mariah has taken some personal time, so I don't have her to talk to in the locker room. Talking to Matt about what I think the day will be like is helpful to get me in the frame of mind I need to be out there. I like having a routine where I can get one. Lord knows this job isn't at all routine.

I knock softly on Matt's door. He's usually here about this time. Matt is a Lieutenant with Gainesville Police Department, but he works during the week. He ends up working with all of our units. I don't know if that's typical, but since we have issues with lazy cops, I'm fairly certain it was a position created just for him.

Matt doesn't take shit from anyone. If he sees something, like an officer who takes significantly less calls then his partner, he'll call it out and deal with it. He's the upper commanding officer's dream. Those that follow the rules love him. But those who like to cut corners absolutely don't.

"Yeah?" Matt calls gruffly. It's then I realize that he had been talking to someone.

I crack the door just a little, but don't enter. "I didn't realize you were talking to someone," I say softly. "I'll come back." I start to close the door.

"Lyric. You can come in, baby. It's just me," DJ says.

I let out a relieved breath as I quietly slip inside Matt's office and close the door. "I didn't mean to interrupt." I blush shyly.

"It's okay," Matt says. "What are you doing here? Aren't you off today?"

I sit in the chair next to DJ. "Yeah. But Sergeant Jackson called me in. And I kind of wanted the overtime."

DJ raises an eyebrow. "You hate overtime."

I smile. "I know. But I have a reason."

"What is it?" Matt asks.

I laugh and look up at him through my lashes. "It's a secret."

"Secret?" DJ chuckles. "We don't do secrets."

I bite my lip. I've never been good at keeping secrets, but this is one that I need to. At least until I can save up the money I need to. "I know. But this is one I'm keeping close to my heart."

Matt and DJ share a look and smile. I furrow my eyebrows as Matt slowly stands. He walks to his door and locks it. I watch him curiously. He slowly walks towards me. I'm entirely focused on him as he places his hands on both arms of the chair I'm sitting in. His already dark and intense eyes seem to get darker as he leans into me. I swallow hard.

"I hate secrets." His already deep voice lowers an octave and vibrates through my whole body, though he's not even touching me.

"It's a good secret," I whisper. His powerful spicy scent envelopes me.

He gives me a cocky half-smile. I know he knows exactly what he's doing to me. He says nothing as he runs his large hands down my arms. He takes my hands in his and pulls me up. Matt and DJ are both tall and muscular men. Compared to me, they both look a little like giants. They could wrap completely around me, and I probably wouldn't even be able to be seen. I love it.

Matt turns me slightly and starts unhooking my gun belt. I want to ask what he's doing, but my throat is suddenly very dry. I forget how to swallow. It's possible I forget how to breathe. All I'm focused on is him. His fingers working the button on my pants and pushing my zipper down. I feel my pants slide down my thighs as he caresses my hips and slowly walks me backwards, effectively helping me step out of my pants.

My boots are still on. As is my shirt. I catch my breath when I feel another solid body behind me. I had almost forgotten DJ was in the room, but when I feel his solid chest at my back and lips on my neck, I whimper quietly.

Matt's thumbs hook my panties. He pulls them down slowly as he kneels in front of me. He kisses my thighs on the way down. I let my head fall back against DJ's shoulder. I've been with both of them individually over the past couple of weeks. I've messed around with both of them at the same time. But something about today feels far more intense. Dangerous. Maybe it's because we're in the police station, locked in an office. We could still be interrupted at any time.

DJ nips my neck at the same time Matt bites the inside of my thigh just below my now bare pussy. I inhale sharply and moan, tangling my fingers in Matt's hair. I reach behind me and grip DJ's thigh. DJ slides his hands slowly up my body under my shirt. He pushes my bra up and grips both of my tits. He kisses across the back of my neck until he reaches the other side. He nips my neck again and squeezes my tits at the same time Matt's tongue dives into my pussy.

"Oh!" I squeak as my eyes roll back in my head.

Matt bites my pussy. "Quiet, baby. Don't get us in trouble."

I let go of DJ as I arch into Matt. I clamp a hand over my mouth and moan. I would fall if DJ wasn't holding me up. Matt spreads my legs while DJ teases my nipples. He squeezes and pinches them, rolling them between his fingers. I tighten my grip on Matt's hair and tug him into my pussy, silently begging him for more.

He doesn't leave me waiting. Matt's tongue is just as magical as DJ's and Mariah's. He knows how to use it. He darts it in and out of my pussy and swirls it around while he sucks. He starts rubbing my clit as I move my hips back and forth over his tongue. My ass hits DJ's very hard dick, making him moan low into my neck.

"Matt," I whisper. "I'm gonna... Please..."

He pinches my clit. I can feel him smiling against my pussy. He rubs my clit faster, giving me the perfect pressure. "Tell me the secret," he says deeply. His voice vibrates into my pussy. It's like he's sending an electrical current through my entire body.

My thighs tremble. "Matt... Please. I'm gonna come..." I know I won't last much longer.

"Not until you tell us what we want to know," DJ whispers in my ear. His voice is deeper than Matt's. More of a drawl. It vibrates throughout my blood directly to my clit. He rubs my nipples and squeezes my tits, pushing himself against my ass.

I gasp. "Oh God." I pull Matt's hair and clamp a hand over my mouth again when I scream as he bites my pussy again before thrusting his tongue deep inside it. "Matt!"

"Tell me the secret, baby," Matt moans into my pussy as he lightly slaps my clit.

I jerk into him hard. My pussy pulses and clenches tightly around his tongue. "Please. Oh God. Please let me come, Matt. Please."

DJ slaps my tits at the same time Matt slaps my clit again. "Tell us, sexy girl," DJ drawls against my neck.

"I'm planning a surprise for everyone. Please don't make me spoil it. Please, please, Matt. Please let me come!"

I can feel him smile against my pussy again. "What do you think, DJ?"

My pussy pulses uncontrollably. My entire body trembles. I'm just about to start begging because I know I'm not going to be able to hold on. I've already been punished once for coming before being given permission. The punishment DJ gave was just as delicious as Matt's tongue, but I'd prefer to not get spanked and teased relentlessly before I'm allowed to come.

The last time, DJ spanked me while Matt fingered me. I didn't get to come for an entire hour while DJ brought me to the edge multiple times beforehand. When I finally got my release, I came so hard, I almost passed out.

DJ's lips start moving against my ear. "Such a good girl for us, aren't you?"

I nod. "Your good girl," I whisper.

"Come for us, baby girl." Matt nips my pussy. I arch as he thrusts his tongue back into my pussy while opening his mouth.

DJ holds me against him with one arm and puts a hand over my mouth. I'm shaking too badly to be able to do it myself. I scream into DJ's hand as I come into Matt's mouth. I buck when I feel his moan vibrate through my pussy. My hips jerk violently with the force of my release. My pussy pulses erratically as he softly starts licking me clean.

After a few moments, DJ releases my mouth as he softly kisses my neck. Matt kisses my pussy after I've come down. He pulls my panties back up and helps me into my pants. I barely feel him pull them up and stand. I pant into DJ's chest as he holds me.

"Oh my God," I whisper as feeling slowly starts to come back to the rest of my body. I open my eyes.

Matt smiles his sexy and very cocky smile. "I told you. Not God, but close."

I giggle and playfully swat him. "So arrogant."

"I know." He winks and presses against me. He tangles his fingers in DJ's hair and kisses him with a low moan.

"Holy fuck… So hot." I bite my lip with wide eyes.

Matt grins when he pulls back. "Thought you'd like to taste her, too."

DJ slowly lets go of me. He looks down and kisses my cheek as I blush. "So fucking sweet."

I moan quietly and look at them both through my lashes as I start putting my uniform back together. I tuck my shirt back in and smooth out the wrinkles as they both watch me. I groan when I see the time.

"It's almost time for turnout," I say quietly.

DJ chuckles. "I'd like to keep you, but we really are short today. We're down three cops even with you out there. Matt and I were just talking about how we are probably going to have to spend some time on the streets today. We were discussing what districts to take."

My heart flutters a little at the thought of them both being out there with me. I love working with Mariah, but with her being off and this being an overtime shift, I'll be out there with a bunch of officers I'm not used to.

As I start putting my gun belt back on, a thought occurs to me. "Why is Sergeant Jackson on today?"

"Because we're down a Sergeant today, too," Matt responds. "He wasn't too happy he was called in either. When I got here, he was slamming shit around by the coffee pot. I think he broke the maker. I was going to check, but DJ caught me."

"So he's in a foul mood." I roll my eyes. "Great."

DJ laughs. "Don't let him fuck with you."

"I'll try not to." I smile at them both. "I feel like I should be repaying you for that. I was not expecting it."

Matt chuckles and takes my chin between his fingers. "You don't have time, honey." He leans down and kisses me.

When he pulls away, DJ leans down and kisses me. He swats my ass when he pulls away. "Go, sweet girl. We'll see you out there later."

I giggle and lightly brush my fingertips over their dicks as I head for the door. They groan in unison. "Oh." I turn as I open the door. "Mariah wanted me to say hi. She knows you both are worried about her. She said she's trying. And…" I smile softly. "And we had some time last night together. She didn't cry or get sick this morning. She actually made me breakfast and a latte. She even kissed me goodbye."

Matt's and DJ's smiles say all they need to. They're proud of her. I close the door quietly behind me. Truth is, I am, too. She's come really far within the past couple of weeks. I can only hope that she'll continue.

I can't wait for her to experience the kind of euphoric bliss that I just did.

Chapter Seven

☆ Matt ☆

I yawn as I submit my last report and look at the time. I really should be out helping patrol, but with the amount of work I had to do, it just hasn't quite worked out that way. At least DJ was able to get out there. I don't feel so guilty about them being down so many people.

Just as I'm about to stand, my phone rings. I smile when I see the name. "Hey, Rih. How's my girl?"

"Um…"

I chuckle as I lean back in my chair. I know she's blushing. "Forget what you called for?"

"No… I just…" She takes a breath. "It's just really nice. Hearing that, I mean."

I smile and lean forward on my desk. "Honey, I've called you my girl before."

"I know. I know you did. But it just feels a little different. Before there wasn't really a commitment, you know? Now, it's like I really feel like your girl."

"I am committed to you." My heart quickens a little bit saying those words. It's like they're words I've wanted to say my entire life. "So? What do you need, baby? It's not often you call while I'm working."

"Right. Um… I was actually just wondering if maybe you'd like to have a movie night with me. DJ asked Lyric and I if we wanted to go see a play. Lyric has never seen the one he wants to go to, but I don't like it so I decided I didn't want to go."

"Sure. If you want me to. I can grab some dinner if you want."

"I'd like that."

"I could leave now. I don't have anything else going on. I planned on leaving early anyway today. We're short, but I'm not feeling so great."

"Okay. Lyric had planned to go right over to DJ's after work. I'm sort of getting a little bored…"

I can't hide the grin. Even though I don't feel well. "I think I can come up with a few ways to help you out with that."

She giggles adorably. "I know you can. I might be counting on that. But if you aren't feeling well, we can just cuddle."

The sexy tease in her voice makes me groan. My cock is already hardening. "Fuck, Mariah. You're going to kill me."

She laughs. "Please. I know you well enough to know you could go all day if you wanted. Sick or not."

"While that may be true, walking out of here with the hard on I'm sporting isn't exactly ideal. So, unless you want to help me out with that…" I trail off with a teasing smile on my lips and my hand very lightly squeezing my dick.

"Hmm… I think maybe you should hurry up and come over here. Since it's only around three, you can skip takeout. We can order in later."

I'm already on my feet before she finishes talking. "Be there in twenty." I hang up to Mariah giggling.

I quickly shut my computer down and grab my gear. I stride to my truck and jump in as soon as I get to it. Mariah's promise is doing things to me that only two other people have the ability of doing. My whole body reacts to her. Her voice is honestly like music to my ears. It has the power to calm me; make me want her like I've only wanted Lyric and DJ.

I kick myself everyday that I waited this long to have the conversation we had regarding our relationship. I have never been happier than I am right now. I feel whole. I don't feel like part of me is missing anymore. I'm not trying to fill a void. I don't feel like I'm looking for anything anymore. I have all I want. Finally.

When I get to Mariah's apartment building, my mood lessens slightly. I have never really been a fan of the apartment complexes in Gainesville. It doesn't seem to matter the neighborhood they are in. I always see the same issues. Shady fuckers. Many who I've dealt with at one time or another. Drugs. Gangs. Flashers. Stalkers.

Looking at Mariah's building, I can see signs that the same issues are running alight here. Even though she and Lyric insist it's a far better choice than what they came from. I chuckle at the crack pipe hiding in the bushes by the door. The cigarette butts scattering the sidewalk instead of in the stone garbage bin labeled for cigarette butts annoys me. It shows laziness and a lack of caring on both the resident's and management's parts. It looks like we'll be having a conversation about living arrangements because I'm not letting either of my girls live in this shit.

Making my way to Mariah's apartment doesn't change my mind. I can hear someone yelling. The floor doesn't look like it's been swept. There's a guy sitting outside a door knocking on it. He looks high as fuck.

When I get to her hallway, I notice it's quiet. It's the top floor. But the carpet still doesn't look like it's been vacuumed. There's crumpled and torn paper littering the floor. There's a cigarette butt a couple of doors down from hers. I shake my head as I knock.

Thank fuck it doesn't take her long to answer. I suck in a breath when I see her. "My God."

She smiles so brightly she could rival the Florida sun. "Are you going to come in? Or gawk?"

I quickly step in and close the door, locking it behind me. I drop my gear and remove my backup shoulder holster. I hate it. I prefer the one I use on my hip, but it's worn out and broke on me. I have to wait for the replacement to arrive and am stuck with this one until that happens.

I hang the shoulder holster on her coat rack. I turn and grab her around the waist. I lift her so she has no choice but to lock her legs around my waist. She squeals as she wraps around me, but I cut it off when I crash my lips to hers.

I kiss her deeply, twinning my tongue with hers. She moans into the kiss and tightens her legs around my waist and arms around my shoulders. The dance is just as hot as it is familiar. I'll never get tired of kissing her, or touching her. I'll never get sick of her reaction to me.

I sit down on the couch, shifting her so she's straddling me. She presses her pussy against me as she spreads her legs further and rubs against me. She deepens the kiss until we're both fighting for the upperhand.

"Tell me you don't answer the door like this for fucking anyone," I growl as I grip her ass. She's wearing nothing but panties that show off her ass and a hoodie that barely covers her pussy. The front of it is cut down her chest so the mounds of her tits are just showing.

She shakes her head. "Absolutely not, Lieutenant." She nips my lip before pressing her lips to mine again.

It's my turn to moan into her kiss. I grip her ass under her panties and contemplate tearing them. Eventually, I decide not to because she looks far too fucking sexy in them to allow myself to ruin them.

I kiss down her neck and reach down to unbutton my jeans. One good thing about being a Lieutenant. I can wear whatever I want unless I have a meeting with an upper level commanding officer or something. Wearing a suit to work every day would piss me off.

I grip my dick and pull it out as I nip her neck and suck. She grips my shoulders and leans her head to the side, giving me more access to her sweet as sin skin. I've never understood why, but Mariah tastes like caramel or something. It has to be her body wash, but I've never asked. I've always been too busy enjoying the way she tastes.

Mariah jumps when my phone goes off. I kiss her neck. "Ignore it." I kiss along her throat as I give my dick a couple of pumps.

"What if it's important?" She gasps when I lick her throat.

"It's not. See? It stopped." I push her panties aside and position her over my dick.

"It could be."

"They'll leave a voicemail."

I run my dick through her wet pussy with a low groan. She drops her head to my shoulder and kisses my neck as she spears my hair. I can feel her anticipation in the way she's already trembling for me. As I sink my dick slowly and deeply into her tight pussy, I think for the millionth time what an idiot I am for not giving her the commitment she wanted long ago. As soon as we talked and I gave her that, she opened up to me like I'd been begging her to for almost four whole fucking years.

And she can't get enough of me. Like I could ever get enough of her. Fuck. Never.

"Oh… God. Matt…," she breathes against my neck as her pussy pulses around my dick while she adjusts to my size.

Mariah is a tiny girl. The first time we were together I couldn't fit all the way inside her. Ten inches is no match for how tight my girl is. I hadn't really expected it. Being small doesn't always mean also being tight. But holy fuck. Mariah surpassed all of my expectations.

I growl at my phone when it rings a second time. "They can wait."

"Matt."

"Mariah. I have been waiting all day for you. I miss you. Whoever that is can wait."

She gives me a shy smile as I slowly begin to move inside her. I grip her hips and thrust just the way she likes. Deep. She wraps her arms around my shoulders and buries her face in my neck. She moves her hips slowly over my dick, setting the pace.

I wrap my arms around her with a smile into her neck. Mariah is not like most of the girls I've been with. Not even like Lyric. She's submissive in a way, which I love. But she likes the slow pace. She likes deep and hard thrusts. She loves my arms around her, holding her as close to me as I can. She likes feeling the closeness.

My phone chimes with a text, but I ignore it. I'm starting to think it really is important, but I can feel how much Mariah needs this. Just as much as I do. I refuse to answer the phone and make her feel like she's not one of the most important people in my world. Because she is. She's everything to me. She's one part of my entire universe.

She starts to tighten around me. "Mmm… Matt…" She kisses my neck and leaves her lips against it as she moans.

I kiss her shoulder up to her neck. "Mariah," I whisper low as she moans.

She clenches tighter with a higher pitched moan. "I…"

She doesn't need to say it. I can feel she's ready. "Come, baby. Come for me." I tangle my fingers in her hair and tug lightly so she looks at me. I'll let her control certain things, like the speed, but one thing I won't give up is watching her come.

She closes her eyes and lets out a breathy moan as she rocks herself over my dick. I keep thrusting. "Matt!" She digs her nails into my shoulders as her release hits her. She clenches around my dick so tightly that I couldn't move if I wanted to. Her hips jerk against mine.

After a couple moments of feeling her pussy pulsing as she comes, I bury myself deep inside her. "Fuck, Mariah." I come hard. My hips meet hers as they start jerking. My dick twitches inside her with each spurt of my come.

As she always does, Mariah blushes a beautiful shade of pink when she realizes I'd been watching her. I smile and lean in. I kiss her as I slowly thrust us both through our releases. She sighs content when I slowly stop thrusting.

My phone starts ringing again. Mariah reaches for it. "Really. It has to be important. You need to take it."

I sigh and take the phone. Seeing DJ's name makes my heart skip a beat. And not because of the way the man makes me feel. No. This is different. Slightly fearful. DJ wouldn't keep calling and texting me. He'd leave a message or a text and leave it alone.

I dread answering, but I do. "Hey, DJ. What's -"

"Get to the hospital. Now. University. It's Lyric."

The panic I'd felt start to bubble to the surface clenches my heart and squeezes. I look at Mariah. "What happened?"

"I don't know. She called in a traffic stop. Next thing I hear is her calling for an ambulance. She said officer down. I rushed to the scene. I don't know where the car she was stopping was, but Lyric was unconscious behind the wheel. She must have passed out after making the call. She crashed into a fucking building."

"Fuck," I say scrubbing a hand down my face. I hadn't even realized that Mariah had gotten up until I hear a crash coming from her bedroom. "We'll be there."

"I tried calling you both." I can hear the accusatory note in his tone.

"Don't. Just fucking don't say it." I hang up and shakily pack myself away as I get up. "Mariah?"

She runs out of the room directly into me. I barely catch her before she falls. "He tried calling me, too! I knew you should have answered." Tears are streaming down her face.

I wrap her in my arms because I need her to steady me as much as she needs me to anchor her. "I know. But there's nothing we can do now but get there, baby."

She wraps her arms around me and takes a deep breath, though she's shaking. "I'm so sorry! I put my own needs above her when she needed us!"

"Fuck, baby. No. Stop it. We didn't know. She'll be okay. We just need to get there, okay? You need to be strong for me, Rih. I can't do this without you." Tears I didn't know I was crying hit her neck as I bury my face in her hair.

She takes another deep breath, breathing in my scent to calm her just as I'm doing with her. "Okay. Okay. We... we need to go. We need to find out what happened. We need to know if Lyric is okay."

I nod and take her hand. We're both trembling, but we rush to my truck. I take off as we're both strapping ourselves into our seatbelts. Mariah grips my thigh so I can drive. It's all I can do to concentrate on the road. All I can think about is Lyric and getting to her. Stopping for red lights is painful, but I do it because I don't want to kill either of us trying to get to the hospital.

While in reality, the drive only takes ten minutes, it seems far longer. I speed into the lot and park near the Emergency Room entrance where I would typically park my squad. I don't even care if my truck gets towed from the area. All that matters right now is getting us to Lyric.

"She's in room eight," Mariah says after reading her texts from DJ.

I nod and take her hand. I pull her along with me. Mariah grips my hand, almost running to keep up with me. I give her hand a squeeze and stop abruptly when someone comes running by with a gurney. Mariah runs into my back. I feel her grip my arm and squeeze my hand.

"If it weren't for you, I'd be losing grip with reality," I whisper as I look around frantically for anyone who can direct me to room eight.

She caresses my arm. "Let me," she whispers back. She pulls me to a nursing station. I let her because I'm doing all I can to slow my racing heart. If this is what Mariah's panic attacks feel like, I don't fucking want them. "Hi. We're looking for room eight. Lyric Sharpe. We're with Gainesville P.D. She's our partner."

"Yes, officer," the nurse says. She gets up and immediately leads us back to the rooms.

"Smart," I say. She smiles as we follow.

Saying that we're Gainesville P.D. instead of just that we're Lyric's boyfriend and girlfriend definitely gets us in quicker. I hate to say that in the state of mind I'm in, I wouldn't have thought to do it. I would have tapped into the dominant Alpha that I am and forced my way in.

The nurse stops outside Lyric's room and looks at us. "She's okay. Bumps and bruises. But she's awake. One of your other partner's is in there with her questioning her about what happened."

I nod. "Thank you, ma'am."

She steps aside and lets us in. She closes the curtain behind us. DJ is sitting with her on the bed and hugging her as tightly as he dares. His head is buried in her hair as he sways gently with her. Lyric is crying quietly and gripping the waistband of his pants.

Mariah and I waste no time. We both sit on the other side of the bed and surround Lyric. Mariah burrows into her. I wrap my arms around everyone. I kiss the back of Lyric's neck and sway soothingly with all of us.

"What happened, baby?" I whisper against her neck.

"I really don't know," Lyric whispers back with a sniffle. "The ABS light was on in the squad I was assigned. But I was told that it was just stuck on. The brakes had been fixed. They were going to take it in and have it reset." She turns her head slightly and nuzzles into Mariah's neck. "I hadn't had a problem all day. I didn't think anything of it. But I was doing a traffic stop. The girl I was stopping must have gotten scared or something when she saw my lights. She slammed on her brakes. I hit mine hard, but..." I feel her body start trembling as she sobs.

"It didn't respond," I whisper.

She shakes her head then freezes, holding her hand to her head with a whimper. "I panicked and jerked the wheel. I didn't want to hit the girl. I tried to stop, but... I couldn't."

"So you hit a building," Mariah whimpers.

"I was aiming for a tree, but at the last second, I saw someone walking. So I went for the side of the building and hoped I didn't go through the wall."

"Thank fuck you didn't go through the wall," DJ mumbles. "I'm fucking going to kill Jackson."

I tug his shirt in warning. I give him a stern look and barely perceptible shake of my head over Lyric's shoulder. Understanding, he gives me a slight nod as we all go back to hugging our girl.

But DJ is right. Sergeant Jackson is going to answer for this. And he better pray DJ gets to him before I do.

Chapter Eight

☆ Mariah ☆

(Two Days Later)

I pace anxiously around DJ's living room, tugging on my hair and sniffling. I twist my hair around my finger and let it go. I do it again and tug before letting it go again. I stop by the stairs and look up before going back to pacing again.

It's been a couple of days since Lyric's wreck. She's doing very well, but she's sore. Matt and DJ gave her a choice. Either stay with Matt or with DJ, but they didn't want either of us home by ourselves.

I agreed. I hated the idea of being away from them. I felt like we all needed to be together. I still feel that way. I don't like the idea of them being away from us when Lyric needs them. Or if she needs something that I can't help her with.

I sigh and sit down in an oversized chair in DJ's living room. I tap my foot against the stool in front of me. I don't really know why I'm so anxious, but I can't sit still. My mind is racing. I don't like Lyric out of my sight. I can't exactly watch her sleep all day. Or hover when she showers.

And there seems to be my problem. Lyric is in a lot of pain. She ended up with a concussion. Her ribs are bruised. Her chest is bruised. She's on the mend, but I hate that it happened in the first place. She's needed help standing up from the bed. She's needed help laying down. Sometimes, when she wakes up, she can't breathe.

I sniffle and stand up. I start pacing again. I hate not knowing what to do. I don't like the fact that I don't know what happened. Everything. Not just bits and pieces. It doesn't make sense to me. How could she be put into a vehicle that had problems? Sergeant Jackson gets a list of usable squads. DJ said that. So how could he put her in a vehicle that was not supposed to be used?

It's like the day he tried to put me into a vehicle that stalled out. He knew that the vehicle wasn't usable. How dare he try and overrule his commanding officers? I twirl my hair around my finger and tug again. How could he be so careless?

"You know, if you tug your hair any harder, you're going to pull it out."

I turn so quickly towards the sliding glass door leading out to DJ's pool, I nearly fall over. I put my hand on the back of the couch to catch myself as I inhale sharply. Matt is leaning against the door frame with his arms folded over his chest.

"Jesus, Matt. You should wear a bell."

He laughs and comes into the house. He closes the door behind him. I watch him as he walks towards me. He's wearing nothing but swim trunks. His skin is perfectly golden. The tattoos that cover his arms make him look like a badass, but Matt is anything but. At least when it comes to me, Lyric, and even DJ. While we've all been taking care of Lyric, Matt has been taking care of us all. Making sure we eat and get outside.

He reaches out and gently grips my arms. "You need to stop pacing, baby. I've been watching you for an hour while I was drying off after my laps. You need to breathe. Lyric is going to be okay."

I sigh and deflate slightly. "It's not that. Well, it is. I am worried about her, obviously, but it's not all that."

"Then tell me, honey. Talk to me. Let me help."

I lean into him and wrap my arms slowly and tightly around his waist. He pulls me close and hugs me just as tightly. "It's Sergeant Jackson. This isn't the first time he's messed up like that…"

"He'll face the consequences. Don't worry about that. But what do you mean that isn't the first time?"

"That day that I showed up with DJ for the bust and you were with Lyric. He told me when I was getting ready to go out that my squad was by the door. I was telling him that I was heading to a call out and was meeting DJ, but he was yelling at me. DJ came out about that time. I told him that I would follow him in my squad and pointed to the one by the door. DJ said that he'd told Jackson I was supposed to be in his squad and Lyric was supposed to be in yours because our squads were down. He said the squad he wanted to put me in stalls out and dies."

"Fuck... Are you joking?"

I shake my head and hug him tighter. "No. I was pretty shaken. I'd forgotten about it. It didn't seem like the most important thing. And I know that DJ wrote him up for that."

Matt kisses the side of my head. "DJ didn't tell me that."

"And a few days ago? Lyric told me that she ended up going back to Headquarters because the squad felt shaky. Another Sergeant put her in a different one that was okay to use. He said that he didn't know why she'd been put in that one in the first place. It had an issue with the front end. Lyric said that she knew that squad was supposed to go in because she was the one who said that it had a problem. She said Jackson screamed at her that it had been dealt with."

Matt pulls back slightly and looks down at me. "Screamed at her?"

I nod. "I assume just like he screamed at me the day DJ saw it. Lyric hates conflict. You know that. You've seen her cowering when we've yelled in the past. Him screaming at her would scare her. Hell. Anyone speaking in a loud voice makes her nervous sometimes. So, when he screams at her, she'd back down right away. She usually has to pull over somewhere where no one can see her because she's crying as soon as she's in the squad. Me? I have stood up to him a lot, but sometimes, even I back down. It sort of depends on the day I'm having."

I watch Matt's expression darken as his jaw works. He's glaring at the wall behind me. His grip on me tightens a little, but it's more of a protective type of hold. Possessive almost. I stand on my tiptoes and kiss his jaw, but before I can say anything, I hear footsteps coming down the stairs. I turn to see DJ. My heart quickens at the sight and sinks at the same time.

"Before you ask, baby. Lyric is okay. She's settled. She's asleep. She's coming back to her same teasing self. She told me that I need to fuck the anxiousness out of you."

I blush but giggle. "That sounds like Lyric," I say quietly.

DJ leans down and kisses me softly when he reaches us. He drops a hand to my lower back and raises an eyebrow at Matt. "Why are you shooting daggers at the wall?"

Matt blinks and shakes his head like he's coming out of a daze. "Did you know Jackson has been putting Lyric in squads he knows are down? He's been doing it for the last few days. And that he tried to put Mariah in one that he knew was bad? I mean, he's lying to them and telling them that they are okay."

"I knew about him trying to put Mariah in a squad that had an engine problem. And Lyric with this brake issue. But there has been more?"

Matt pulls away with a sigh and runs his fingers through his hair. "Yeah. Fuck. He put her in a car with front end issues. He told her it was fixed. Screamed at her about it when she asked him if it was okay. She knew something was wrong with it because she was the one who pointed out the issue."

I hug myself. "I just don't know what to do about it. It's bothering me. I don't understand. Why would he do that?"

DJ pulls me closer to him. "I don't know, baby. I don't. But you better believe I'm going to find out. He'll be there tomorrow. I'll pull him into my office."

"We can't let him get away with it, DJ. This is cause to be fired." Matt shakes his head and starts pacing himself before he turns back to us. "He can't be allowed to deal with the garage."

"Matt," DJ says as he tightens his grip on my waist. "I'll take care of it. You can deal with the garage tomorrow. I'll talk to who I need to talk to. These things are delicate. The department can't just fire him. There has to be an internal investigation."

Matt scoffs. "DJ, fuck! Come on! That's gross fucking negligence on his part. He could have killed Lyric! And Mariah, for that matter, if you hadn't caught up to her before she left the garage."

I hug myself tighter and take a deep breath. I rub my chest and blink back the tears. I step to Matt. "Please don't yell," I say quietly. "You'll wake Lyric. She didn't sleep well." I gently touch his arm.

Matt nods and kisses my head. "I'll check on her." He scrubs his hand down his face as he climbs the stairs.

DJ watches him before turning back to me and sitting on the couch. He reaches up and takes my hand. "Come here."

I look up the stairs worriedly, but I let him pull me in his lap. "I'm so worried about her."

"I know." He takes my chin in his finger and thumb and gently turns me to face him. "Do you trust me?"

I soften a little. "You know I trust you."

"Then will you trust me when I say she's okay?"

I take a breath. "I don't think my worry truly stems from her. I think I'm scared because of what happened to her. It was totally preventable. Why her? What does Jackson have against -"

DJ cuts me off with a deep kiss that takes my breath away. When he slowly pulls away, I completely forget what I had been saying. I'm sure it's the intention. He tangles his fingers in my hair and tugs gently as he kisses me again.

DJ smiles. "Stop. Stop thinking about it. It's my job to deal with it. You thinking about it is going to drive you crazy. Everything you have going on behind those pretty blue eyes of yours are things I'm already thinking. I promise that I will deal with him."

I smile and nuzzle his jaw. "I just -"

He kisses me again as he grips my waist. He flips me onto my back on the couch and pins my hands above my head. I squeak before he covers my mouth with his again. He deepens the kiss until I feel it in my toes. I close my eyes and submit completely to him. He keeps my wrists above my head as he kisses along my jaw to my throat.

"Stop worrying. Stop thinking about it. Your job is to take care of our girl. You have a few more days off. Use them to help her get her strength back. Let me and Matt deal with Jackson and his bullshit."

I smile and nip his jaw before kissing it. He smiles back and leans down. He kisses my neck and down my collarbone. Still holding my wrists above my head with one hand, he uses his other hand to leave a trail of goosebumps up my thigh. He keeps moving slow and lightly until he reaches the hem of my tank top. He pushes it up with that same slow pace, leaving heat in his wake.

I arch into him and become putty in his hands. My whole body awakens and yearns for him. I'd give anything if it meant him never stopping touching me. His lips are hot against my skin. His hands are just rough enough to cause sensations to run through me that I've never felt with anyone else but Matt. The calluses on his hands from years of training with guns and using his hands for his work bring me a type of delight that makes me crave his caress.

"DJ," I murmur, closing my eyes and letting myself feel.

"Hmm…?" His lips move down to my bra. He nips my nipple just over the soft, silky fabric.

"Oh," I moan as I wiggle against him. He kisses across my chest to my other nipple and nips it as he had the other. "DJ… Oh…" I've lost the ability to form complete sentences. All I can do is breathe and arch into him.

I feel him smile against me as he continues making his way lower. When he reaches the waistband of my jean cut-offs, he lets go of my wrists. He makes quick work of the button and tugs them, along with my panties, slowly off my hips and down my legs.

He kisses from my ankle up my leg, taking turns with each one. When he gets to my upper thighs, I'm pretty sure my entire body is going to erupt in the same vibration he's somehow managed to make my clit do, though he hasn't actually touched it.

"You're already so wet for me, my girl. I haven't even really started yet." His voice makes me tremble. His hot breath makes me erupt in delicious goosebumps and shiver.

Just when I'm about to open my eyes and beg him to relieve the pressure, I feel lips against mine. Only DJ's are still against my thigh just next to where I want him most. Before I have a chance to fully realize what's happening, a pair of strong hands expertly remove my bra. Matt's mouth is on my nipples just as DJ finally finds my clit with his tongue.

"Oh God!" I throw my hand against the back of the couch and grip it with wide eyes.

I've been with DJ and Matt. But I haven't been with them together. My head is saying to slow down. That I have to take back control. But every part of my being refuses to listen. I can't form the words. Instead, the traitorous thing arches into DJ's tongue, pleading for more. My hand, the one that isn't holding on for dear life, grabs onto Matt's arm. It scratches up his arm to his shoulder blade then digs its nails in.

I have no control of it. My body is doing what it wants to. And it has somehow convinced my mind that this is exactly what it wants. There's no logical part of my being now. I'm melting into their touches and teasing caresses with their tongues.

Matt moans deeply against my nipples. DJ moans just as low against my clit. The dual sensations send some kind of electricity all the way to the top of my head. I writhe and moan under them like I'm being slowly electrocuted or something. But if I'm going to die by a slow electrical current, God let it be like this.

"Fuck, Mariah," DJ groans against me before he sucks my clit into his mouth.

"Oh, God!" I can already feel myself getting close. I jerk into his mouth and arch into Matt's tongue. "Oh my God. Matt… DJ!"

Matt chuckles. "We haven't even started with you, baby girl."

My eyes widen just as DJ thrusts his tongue deep into my pussy. I want to scream, but the sensations flowing through me makes all sound die on my tongue. I let my head fall back on a moan. I spear my fingers into Matt's hair and grip the couch cushion harder. My hips jerk uncontrollably to the rhythm of DJ's tongue.

Matt nips my nipple and moves his hand slowly down my body. He starts rubbing my clit at the same pace DJ is tongue fucking me. The tremble that typically starts in my thighs is coursing through my veins. My entire body shivers.

DJ swirls his tongue inside my pussy and moans. Matt nips my nipples again and growls as he rubs my clit in a faster circle. He gives me more pressure while DJ sucks and nips my pussy. I buck into them both, letting out unintelligible whimpers as I try to tell them I'm going to come. I thrash my hand against the cushion and tug on Matt's hair.

When DJ pushes one finger slowly inside me and instantly finds my G-spot, my eyes roll back in my head. I arch off the couch and jerk my hips as I thrust my pussy over DJ's tongue and against his finger.

"I think our girl is ready to come," DJ says deeply. His mouth is still against my pussy. I know he knows that his voice is sending shockwaves through me.

"I think you may be right." Matt sucks my nipple into his mouth before moving to the other. He gives that one the same treatment as he flicks my clit.

"Ah!" I manage to squeak out as I jerk into them both again.

"Come for us, baby," DJ says as he nips my pussy. He thrusts his tongue into me again and again as he crooks his finger relentlessly against my spot.

I claw at the couch, scrambling for purchase as I come harder than I've ever come in my life. My hips jerk as erratically as my pussy clenches and pulses around DJ's tongue. My clit throbs under Matt's touch as I ride wave after wave of the most intense pleasure I've ever felt.

When I finally come down, I realize I've somehow ended up in Matt's lap. My legs are over DJ's. Matt is running his fingers through my hair. DJ is gently rubbing my legs. My body slowly stops trembling as I cuddle into them both.

"That was superbly intense," I whisper into Matt's neck. "I've n-never…" I trail off. I know I don't need to tell them that I've never been with two men at the same time. But I do feel the need to explain the extreme release. I just don't know how. "I've never… come… like that… before."

DJ leans over and kisses me softly. "I gathered." He hands me a bottle of water. "Sip it."

I look at him incredulously. I'm just about to lay into him for making commands like I'm a child or something. But then I realize I'm really fucking thirsty. Instead, I smile softly and do what I'm told.

"Good girl," Matt says, nuzzling my neck.

DJ smiles and squeezes my thigh. "Now. Tell me. Do you feel better? Less anxious?"

I blush furiously but nod. "Yes. Thank you," I say quietly as I hide behind the water bottle.

"You never have to thank us, honey," Matt whispers in my ear.

I smile and blush darker when I realize I don't know where my panties are. Or my shorts. My shirt is still pushed up over my tits, which are hanging out because I'm also no longer wearing a bra. I shift a little uncomfortably under their intense stares.

Before I reach up and pull my shirt down, DJ is already doing it for me. He kisses each of my tits before he kisses me. I smile shyly as Matt kisses my blush.

DJ runs his thumb over my lip. "You're adorable, my shy girl."

I bite my lip as butterflies take flight in my stomach and make their way to my chest. Both Matt and DJ make my heart skip a beat, but the tenderness they show after sex is mind-blowing. I've never had anyone take care of me like they do.

Other than Lyric. Up until recently, every time I was with her, I'd cry afterwards. Because I hated how much I enjoyed her. I thought it made me a bad person. Even though I'm sure it hurt her to know that was my reaction to her, she still took care of me. She wiped my tears when I cried and said it was okay. She held my hair back when I threw up. I had to have made her feel like shit, yet she still took care of me. She made me soup.

"Soup," I say as I start to get up. I put my water on the table. "I'm going to make soup. Lyric deserves the world after the way I treated her."

DJ shakes his head. "What are you talking about?"

Matt smiles. I know he gets it right away. After the long, intimate conversations I've had with him about, I'd be surprised if he didn't understand.

I spot my panties and shorts as I get up. "Whenever I was with her before we all started to admit how we felt about each other, I would cry afterwards. And sometimes throw up. I know how sensitive she is. It had to make her feel so bad, but she still stood by me and took care of me." I wipe my eyes as I pull my panties up. "She waited me out." I pull my shorts up. "It was her way of showing me she loved me all this time. Now, it's my turn."

Matt chuckles. "So, soup will make her see how much you love her?"

I push the straps of my tank top down and push it down to my waist. I pull my bra over my head. "Nope. But it's a start." I tug my bra in place and adjust my tank top as I head for the kitchen. "Soup."

I realize DJ and Matt are watching me, more than amused, but all I care about is making the soup. Lyric needs me to take care of her now. So while the guys deal with the one who hurt her, I'll do just that.

It's time for someone to take care of Lyric for once.

And that someone is going to be me.

Chapter Nine

★ DJ ★

I drum my fingers against my desk as I wait for Chief King to show up. I specifically scheduled this meeting early with him because I want the person who caused harm to my girl to be held responsible so I don't have to resort to some vigilante type of justice. Though, it's not something I'd put past me. Not with the mood I'm in. I called him at home last night. He'd said he'd be here early so we could come up with a plan of action while Internal Affairs investigates Sergeant Jackson's actions.

I have Matt dealing with turnout and squad assignment. I don't want Jackson anywhere near my officers. If I have my way, the fucker will quietly crawl back to the hole he crawled out of and simply go away. After I pummel him and make him look a little like the girl he caused pain to.

"You know, if you drum your fingers any longer on your desk, you might just end up drumming a hole right through the wood."

I smile at Lyric. I asked her if she'd come into the office with me for this meeting because I want the Chief to see her. I want him to see just how fucked up Lyric is right now. How close I was, we were, to losing her.

My request didn't come without argument and pushback from Matt and Mariah. Both want her home and recovering. I couldn't really argue with that. I want her home and recovering, too. But I also know that seeing what he did to her is important. It was a decision I had fought myself on before finally deciding that she needed to be a part of this meeting, so fighting Matt and Mariah both on it wasn't how I wanted to start my morning.

I was close to telling both of them the decision had been made. There was no negotiation about it. No argument. Lyric would be coming with me for this meeting. End of fucking story. That's it.

But Lyric herself is a force to be reckoned with. She also recognized the importance of Chief King seeing with his own eyes what happened to her. Even though she's healing, she's still bruised as fuck. Her face is still swollen. She still has a black eye that is still a very deep purple. Moving is painful for her. Her ribs are wrapped. She has cuts and bruises on her arms, face, and even her neck from where the broken glass struck her.

She limps. It's partially because it hurts her ribs and chest to walk, but also because she tensed when she hit. She was still trying to make the brakes work. She damn near shattered her ankle and knee. Thank all the fucking Gods that she didn't.

Lyric stood up to both of them and said she wanted to go. They both tried to argue with her, but she put her foot down. Literally. She stood next to me with her arms crossed over her chest and stomped her foot, even though I could see it hurt to do so. She told them that she is going and that is her final decision. She said if they tried to stop her, she'd find a way to sneak out and go herself. She said that she knows just how important it is for the Chief to see her right now, so he could understand exactly the damage that was caused.

I smile and shake my head at the thought. "I hate being kept waiting," I say to her.

She giggles quietly. "Don't I know it."

I know she's trying to lighten my mood, but the longer I wait, the more pissed off I become at being kept waiting. I don't want Lyric to be here longer than she has to be. I can see how much pain she's in right now.

"He'll be here soon, DJ." She gives me another soft smile as she blinks sleepily.

The pain pills they put her on make her tired. I truly don't like how much she's struggling, but I keep telling myself that it's for the greater good. It's necessary. If it wasn't, she'd be curled up right now at home tucked in right beside Mariah where she belongs.

I look up at the knock on my door. "Fucking finally," I growl under my breath. "It's open."

"Rens," the Chief says. "Ms. Sharpe." He sits down next to her as he looks her over. "Shit."

"That's not even the half of it." I stand and walk to Lyric. I gently help her up. She whimpers under her breath. I know the Chief didn't hear her, but I sure as hell did. "You still okay showing him?"

She nods slowly. "He needs to see." She takes a breath as she pulls her shirt up. She can't wear a bra, so she only lifts it far enough that the top of the ACE bandage wrapped around her ribcage can be seen.

I push it up a little further, still making sure her tits are covered. "Can you hold that so I can unwrap this?"

"Mmhmm."

Lyric keeps her eyes on me as she hugs herself. She may be very open with me, Matt, and Mariah, but when it comes to showing any part of herself to anyone else, Lyric is incredibly reserved. I know this is making her just as uncomfortable as the high level of pain she's in. So, as I unwrap the bandage, I make sure my eyes don't leave hers. Anything to make her as comfortable as I can.

"Holy shit. Lyric, I'm so sorry," Chief King breathes when he sees her bruises.

I quickly wrap her back up and help her put her shirt down. I smile a little because the shirt she's wearing is mine. She told me she feels more comfortable in larger clothing, so she's been alternating between mine and Matt's clothing the last couple of days. I can't say I mind seeing my girl in my clothes.

"That's not all of it," I say. Knowing she doesn't want to show him more than she has to, I help her sit down. "She has scratches all over her arms from the glass when the windshield shattered. She even has bruising on her legs." I lean against my desk in front of them and cross my arms over my chest as my expression darkens. "She almost shattered her right leg because even though she knew the brakes didn't work, she was trying to hit them anyway."

Lyric hugs herself and tries to curl up in the chair but can't. She bites her lip and looks down at my shoes. "I could've died." She reaches up and wipes away a tear. I kneel in front of her as she bursts into tears. She wraps her arms around me as I gently hug her. "He could've killed me."

I tangle my fingers in her hair as I rock gently with her. "Ssh… It's okay. You're safe, honey," I whisper in her ear. It's the first time she's actually admitted what could have happened to her. "You're safe."

The Chief shakes his head as he rubs his hand across the upper part of Lyric's back as soothingly as he can. But I can see how infuriated he actually is by his grip on the arm of the chair he's sitting in. His jaw is so tense, I actually fear he may break it if he clenches it any harder.

"Now, tell me what happened," he says. "How did she end up in this situation in the first place?"

I don't let go of Lyric as I talk to him. "Sergeant Jackson put her in a squad he knew was out of service. That's the simple answer. The more detailed one is that this particular squad had a brake issue. I had an order put in to have them fixed. I had that squad on the inoperable list."

"I saw. Pulling the list was the first thing I did."

I run my hand up and down Lyric's back soothingly. "This isn't the first time. He tried to put Mariah in a squad with spark plug issues. That vehicle would stall out constantly. He told her that the check engine light was on, but it was a sensor. And he put Lyric in another vehicle that had front end issues. He told her it had been resolved. He screamed at her about it. Told her something like if he says it's okay then it's okay. Lyric took it and brought it right back. Another Sergeant put her in another squad."

The Chief rubs his hands over his face. "Jesus. This ends today. Pull him off the streets. He's not to be on garage duty. I want him on desk duty."

Lyric clears her throat as she slowly pulls away. "Um…" She sniffles and avoids eye contact with both of us. "There's more…"

We both look at her. I stay kneeled in front of her and drop a hand to her thigh. "What do you mean there's more, baby?"

"The squads…" She takes a deep breath and focuses on her hands. "Mariah's first day off. He was upset that he was down a cop. He put me in an unmarked squad that day. I was on a traffic stop. It started to overheat. I had to call for a tow." She sniffles. "A couple days later, he put me in a squad that was really shaky and pulled really badly. I brought it back in. Sergeant Tangs asked me why I was driving that one instead of the one assigned to me. I told him that is the squad Sergeant Jackson put me in." She chews her lip nervously.

I reach up and run my thumb over it. "Lyric, why am I just hearing about this?"

"I didn't want to upset you," she whispers. "I didn't want you to be disappointed in me."

"Lyric. That would never happen, sweet girl." I lean forward and pull her back into my arms.

She breathes a relieved breath. "There was one more incident. I didn't mention this one only because Sergeant Powell laid into Jackson pretty hardcore. But I was on a domestic. I was taking the guy in. Sergeant Powell responded with me because she was close. The car wouldn't start. The guy was being super aggressive. He had been tased during the arrest. I ended up using pepper spray on him during it, too. When we got him in my squad, he was still kicking and screaming." She nuzzles my shoulder and takes another breath. "Sergeant Powell looked into that squad when we had it towed. To see if it was on the inoperable list. That squad had something wrong with the starter. It would start sometimes. Other times it wouldn't. Other officers had complained about it a lot."

The Chief stands and shakes his head. "So, he's put you in how many squads that he knew had problems?"

"Five," I answer for her.

"And that's not counting what he did to Mariah," Lyric whispers.

"How the hell is this happening?" he sighs and sits down, putting his head in his hands. After a few moments, he looks up at me. "I'll contact IA. Have them investigate. We'll put him on desk duty for the duration of the investigation, but only because I want this done quietly."

"Fuck that," I growl. "Fire him."

"I can't, DJ. Not until after the investigation is complete. You know that."

I move to stand, but Lyric doesn't let go. I kiss her neck and pull her up with me. Knowing she needs to sit because standing hurts, I walk her to my chair and sit, pulling her in my lap. It's obvious she doesn't want to be away from me after the realization of nearly being killed just hit her. Truthfully, I'm not that big of a fan of letting her out of my arms either, so I'm not upset in the slightest when she curls up as much as she can and burrows into me.

I look at the Chief. "So, what do you want me to do right now?"

"I want you to put him on the desk. Assign someone else to the garage. Have Chance lead turnout. I'll get the ball rolling with IA. I need statements from both Lyric and Mariah. Also you since you witnessed what happened with Mariah. I want a statement from Sergeant Powell and Sergeant Tangs regarding both incidents with Lyric at the domestic and when she brought the squad back to the garage to be swapped out." He stands and heads for the door. "And Lyric?"

She sniffles and looks up at him. "Yes, sir?"

"I'm glad you're okay. I won't let him get away with this. We'll get to the bottom of it. You just need to give me time to do it right, so he can't come back on us. Accuse us of wrongful termination or something."

She nods. "Thank you, sir."

As soon as he closes the door behind him, Lyric's lips are against mine. She grips my shoulder with one hand and spears my hair with the other. She presses against me with small whimpers that force me to pull back.

"Hey. Hey, baby. Be careful."

But she doesn't. She pulls me to her and kisses me hard. Long. Deeply. Like it's the last kiss she's ever going to get. Her tongue tangles with mine. She tugs my hair and scratches her nails along my shoulder. It's hard not to respond to her. I kiss her back as my cock strains against my jeans, but I still pull back. I grip her wrists.

She fights me slightly, trying to get closer to my lips. "DJ…"

I keep hold of her. "Lyric. What are you doing?"

She sniffles. "I… need you. I can't explain it." She shakes her head as a tear falls. "I need to feel alive. Like I'm… still… here. Like he didn't succeed in whatever sick goal he has to get rid of me." She chokes on a sob that she tries to hold back.

I break. I would never be able to hold back from her, or not give her what she needs. She trembles as she looks pleadingly at me. I lean in and kiss her slowly. I let her wrists go so she can feel me, but keep control of the kiss by tangling my fingers in her hair. She closes her eyes and submits almost instantly when I nip her tongue. I suck gently before pulling away gently. I kiss down her jaw as I undo the button on my pants.

I nudge her up. When she stands, I pull my pants down enough to free my dick. I groan slightly when it springs free because a hard on always hurts if my dick is tucked away. Lyric looks down at me. She bites her lip. I can see she's still trembling a little and fighting tears. I reach over and pull her sweats down. I gently turn her and pull her down on top of me.

"DJ," she whispers as I slide my dick deep into her pussy.

"Ssh… Close your eyes, baby. Feel."

"Yes, sir," she whispers.

I feel the instant she relaxes. I pull her back to me and wrap my arms around her as tightly as I dare but nowhere near enough to hurt her. I start thrusting slowly. She immediately clenches and pulses around me with a soft moan.

I know she wants this hard and fast. I can tell by the way she's trying to move against me. "Lyric." I whisper commandingly in her ear. "I said feel. Let me do the work."

"Yes, sir." She relaxes, submitting once more as I thrust. She wraps her arms around mine and lets her head fall back.

"That's my girl." I kiss her neck and continue thrusting. I hold her still while I move myself inside her. Her erratic clenches and pulses slow and start matching my rhythm.

She moans softly and breathes content sighs as I move my hips against hers. I let her thrust over me, but I won't let her go fast. I press my lips against her neck and fill her completely with each and every thrust.

She keeps hugging my arms tightly to her as she turns her face into mine. She kisses me with soft whimpers as she starts to tighten around me and pant. She keeps her eyes closed and allows herself to feel just like I told her to.

"DJ," she whispers against my lips as she trembles against me and clenches hard.

I kiss her again. I feel her getting closer, so I thrust a little faster; a little harder. I'm constantly mindful of the pain I know she's in. While making sure she gets the pleasure she wants and closeness to me she needs, I hold her still so it's just me moving. I reach down and rub her clit with just the amount of pressure I know she likes. I give her long and deep thrusts.

Her pussy starts to pulse and clench erratically around me. She hugs my arm with one of hers. With her other hand, she reaches down and grips my wrist. She arches into me as much as she can and moans quietly. I smile against her neck.

"DJ… Please…"

I kiss her again when she turns to me. "Come for me, pretty girl."

She comes quietly as she kisses me. I bury my dick as far in her as I can. As her pussy spasms around me, I come hard and deep with her. Keeping my lips against hers and my tongue in a delicious tango with hers to keep her quiet, I empty myself in her. I slow my rubs and thrust her gently through her release.

It takes her a few moments to come down, but when she does, I feel her tears against my neck. I slowly pull out of her and gently nudge her off me. I lean down and pull her sweats and panties back up. I stand and tuck myself away then pull her into my lap again. I push her hair out of her face.

"How's my girl?"

She blushes. "Better. I… don't know why I needed that." She looks down at her hands.

I smile and kiss her forehead. "You don't need a reason. If it's what you needed, and it helps, then I'm happy to do it."

She smiles softly and lays her head on my shoulder. "Thank you."

I run my fingers through her hair and hug her as tightly as I dare. "You don't need to thank me for giving you what you need. It was a scary realization. I don't blame you for needing to feel something other than fear." I kiss her forehead. After a few minutes of hugging her, though, I know I need to get her home. "I hate to let you go, baby, but I have to deal with Jackson. Matt should be in his office by now."

She nods. "He'll be taking me home?"

"Yes. The sooner I can deal with this, the sooner we can move on. I want this shit behind us once and for all."

She smiles as she slowly stands up. "Me, too."

I follow her to the door, keeping my hand on her lower back. I reach around her and open the door. But instead of Lyric moving through it like I expect, she stops cold. I barely stop myself before colliding with her.

When I look up, though, I see why she froze. I clench my fist at my side and let out a low rumbling growl.

Chapter Ten

☆ Lyric ☆

I can't breathe. My vision suddenly blurs. I try to move but can't. I feel like my heart is beating, but it's not pumping blood through my veins. My veins are frozen. My blood is cold. My lungs have collapsed and won't inflate to take in the air I so desperately need. I want to back up into the safety of DJ's office, but my body refuses to obey.

Sergeant Jackson is looking me up and down with a disgusting smirk on his face. Like he's proud of what he'd done. The viciousness in his eyes sends shivers from my head to my toes. I've never felt as much fear of anyone as I do him. And I've lived through violent bullying and abusive relationships. None of that terrifies me as much as Sergeant Jackson's cold stare.

"Sergeant Jackson really wanted to speak to my superior officer," Matt says with a smirk. "He really didn't like my decision to pull him from the garage today and lead turnout myself."

"Is that so?" DJ growls dangerously behind me. His hands drop to my waist.

I shake my head like I'm coming out of the fog clouding my vision. DJ's hands are like my anchor. My safe harbor. I take a deep breath and let myself feel him. I'm safe with him. He won't let anyone hurt me. I watch as Jackson schools his expression quickly when he sees DJ. But I can still see the cold-hearted snake behind the facade.

"Yes, sir, it is so. He can't make that decision," Sergeant Jackson whines.

DJ chuckles. "Lieutenant Chance is your commanding officer. I assure you, he can assign you wherever he wants to. And given your gross negligence lately, I'm inclined to agree with him." He steps back, pulling me with him. "Come inside. Let's talk."

Sergeant Jackson shoots me a withering glare that makes me cringe. I look to my side and focus on DJs arm. I close my eyes and feel his hands at my hips and chest against my back. After a few moments, he guides me forward.

"What's the plan?" Matt asks in a low, gravelly tone. I finally dare to open my eyes.

DJ closes his door and speaks just as low. "I already pulled him from the garage and had you leading turnout. Chief King says he'll contact IA. I need to bench him. No patrol. He's on desk duty. We don't want him aware that IA is investigating this shit. I'll have you deal with the garage today. I need to assign his duties to others."

I bite my lip and stay as close to DJ as possible. "I wish they'd just fire him," I whisper.

"I know, baby. But we need to do this by the book. Chief King is right about that. Be overly cautious about it so he has nothing he can use to fight us," DJ whispers in my ear. He kisses my cheek.

"Ready to head home?" Matt asks.

I shiver against DJ, suddenly feeling extremely vulnerable and not wanting to let him go. I turn into his chest and take a deep breath. His fresh and earthy scent fills me, but my heart still races. I sniffle, feeling ridiculous.

DJ kisses the top of my head. "I know how scared you are, honey. But you're just as safe with Matt as you are with me. You know that, baby." He keeps his lips in my hair as he talks low enough for only me to hear. He hugs me tightly.

I nod. "I know…"

Matt steps closer to me so I feel his body heat. He holds out a hand. I take a shaky breath and take it. His large, strong hand closes gently around mine. I reach up and clutch his arm. I lean against him.

"I won't let anyone touch you, Lyric," he whispers in my ear. "But we need to get you home, baby."

I nod and let him lead me away from DJ. I don't let go of his hand or his arm. I keep my head down so my hair falls in front of my face. I don't want to see anyone. I just want to get out of here. It's still early enough that no one is here. The only reason the Chief was is because DJ called him. Sergeant Jackson was because Matt called him.

When we get to Matt's truck, he helps me in. He pulls the seatbelt for me and buckles me in, kissing me. I hug myself and keep my head down as he closes the door. He quickly walks around to the driver's side and jumps in.

It was only seconds, but in that time, I've already managed to have several flashbacks to my younger years. So many different times when I thought I was going to die at the hands of either my bully tormentors or my ex. They all speed through my mind at record speeds I can't keep up with. By the time Matt sits down, I'm hyperventilating.

"Holy shit, baby," Matt says. When his arms wrap around me, I burst into tears.

"It just brings back everything from my past! The cold way he looked at me. Like he didn't care at all! It was like everyone who bullied me and my ex all over again!"

"Ssh… It's okay, beautiful. You're okay. You're completely safe. I'm not letting him near you." He kisses my neck sweetly as he tangles his fingers in my hair and hugs me as close as he can to him.

"I don't want to work here anymore if he's going to be here." I let myself cry into his solid shoulder as he protectively holds me.

"He's not going to be working here much longer. By the time you get cleared to come back, he'll be gone, baby girl. I promise. We just need to do this by the book. We don't want him to come back and say we fired him without doing a proper investigation." He sways gently with me and speaks against my neck. "Truth is, we're taking a lot of extra precautions. We could charge him now with attempted murder, but we're allowing IA to do their job. We're allowing them to investigate to prevent it from coming back on us. He can't turn around and say that we acted rashly because of our involvement with you. It's the reason DJ went to the Chief instead of making the desk duty assignment himself or suspending the fucker. He wanted the backup."

I take a deep breath. Matt's spicy cologne has the same effect on me that DJ's fresh one does. It's calming. It makes me feel safe. Protected. Like in order to get to me, any kind of danger has to get through him. My very own, personal, impenetrable force.

I wipe my eyes as I slowly pull away. Matt kisses my cheek and reaches up to wipe my tears away. I smile softly and lean into his hand more than appreciative that he can read me well enough to know not to let go of my hand. He kisses me softly. I keep his hand in my lap and grip his arm as he starts to drive.

"Do you think he'll be there for long?" I ask quietly, playing with his fingers.

"No. I don't. I think IA will complete the investigation pretty quickly. Cops may not like getting IA involved. They may very well be the most hated of cops. But one thing I will say about them is they don't fuck around when it comes to the safety of other cops. They'll give us a recommendation, and we'll act."

I sniffle. "What if they don't find anything in their investigation? What if he wipes records or something? What -"

"Baby, stop. Breathe." He brings my hand to his lips and kisses my fingers. "Take a breath."

I rub my chest and take a breath. "It just scares me."

"I know it does. I can see it. But, honey, there's so many unanswered questions. Why is he going after you? Why Mariah? I mean, this started with Mariah. But with her being off, it seems like he's refocused his attention on you."

"Why is he focused on us in the first place?"

"Exactly. It doesn't make sense. I've never dealt with this kind of situation. That's why I'm being as protective as I am."

I focus on my hand in his, He's put it over his heart. I can feel his heart beating. Steady and strong. Just like Matt. I nervously chew on my lip as my mind tries to focus but runs away with me instead. I hate that I don't know what Sergeant Jackson's play is. I don't understand why he's targeting me and Mariah. It's unsettling not knowing.

Matt pulls into DJ's garage, and I can't help breathe a sigh of relief. We've only been here a few days, but it feels like home. I feel comfortable here. Like this is where I belong. Add in that Matt and Mariah are also staying here, it makes everything perfect. Like the four of us are the completion to some grand scheme that was set in motion long ago.

Matt helps me down from his giant truck and kisses me as my feet hit the floor. I smile into the kiss and wrap my arms around him. He holds me against the truck in such a way that I couldn't move if I wanted to, but also so he's not hurting me. He deepens the kiss successfully making me forget all thoughts running through my mind. All I'm focused on is him.

His hands on my hips.

His tongue tangling with mine.

Just him.

When he finally pulls slowly away, he's smirking. "Better?"

I look up at him dazed. "What?"

He smiles wider. "Good."

I giggle and swat his arm. "I don't know what just happened, but I'm all wet."

He laughs. "I'll gladly help you out with that later. Right now, I need to deliver you to Mariah and get my ass back to work before DJ spanks me."

I crack up as he leads me in the house. "The best thing about that statement is I can actually see him spanking you."

"No. The best part of that statement…" He turns to me and bends to whisper in my ear. "Is that I'd like it." He kisses my neck as I suck in a breath at the thought of him being spanked by DJ.

I let out a soft whimper and cross my legs. "You're awful."

He chuckles when he sees my legs are crossed. "I know." He leans down and kisses me before leading me the rest of the way in the house.

Mariah smiles from the kitchen. "How did it go?"

"Pretty well. Until Sergeant Jackson showed up and looked me up and down like he was proud of what he'd done." I shake my head.

Mariah glares. "I wonder how he'd feel with a ten foot pole stuck up his ass."

Matt laughs. I just blink as I sniff the air, trying to figure out what Mariah is cooking. Matt leans down and kisses Mariah just as deeply as he did me by the truck. Her moan forces me to look away. Not because of jealousy or anything stupid like that. But because her moan and the sexiness of that kiss is like watching porn. I'm already close enough to coming.

I bite my lip and focus on the smell. Something sweet. Maybe a little savory. Absolutely smelling bacon. And maple. And vanilla. I sniff again. Caramel? I make my way into the kitchen just as Matt pulls away slowly from Mariah. He whispers something in her ear that makes her giggle before he drops a sweet kiss on my neck. I smile.

"I need to get going," Matt says. "But maybe if you ask nicely, Mariah will do something about that throb between your thighs."

My eyes widen, and I blush a dark shade of red. "Matt!"

He laughs. "I'll see you both later." He heads back out.

I shake my head. "He's so bad."

Mariah giggles. "Too sexy for his own good."

I smile and turn to her. "So what are you making? There's so much stuff out."

"Oh… Um…" She looks around at her mess. "I'm making fudge and ice cream."

I look at her in awe. "I don't think I've ever made homemade fudge or ice cream."

"It's maple bacon fudge and maple bacon ice cream. I think it might be a Minnesota thing. Or at least an up North thing. I don't think I've ever seen it down here. Then again, I haven't been to the State Fair or anything since I moved here."

"I've never had maple bacon fudge or ice cream."

Mariah smiles and holds a spoon up to my mouth. "Try. It's the batter I'm using for the ice cream."

I give her a hesitant look but take a small taste. "Oh my God." I eagerly lick the rest of what's on the spoon as she smiles brightly. "It's so good!"

She claps excitedly. "Yay! I was hoping you'd like it." She takes another spoon and makes me try something else. "It's the fudge. Not set yet, but try."

I smile at her happiness. "It's really, really good. But what made you decide to cook all this?"

"I needed to do something. I looked up a recipe and decided to try it." She pulls something out of the oven. "I also made your favorite."

My smile brightens when I see the dish. "You made hash browns with bacon, mushrooms, eggs, and cheese?"

"Mmhmm. With black olives. And I threw tomatoes in for me, but I didn't put them in yours."

"I love these. I haven't had them in so long. Damn DJ for making them become an addiction so long ago. And omelets! So good!"

"You can go sit down, my love. Get comfortable. I just need to put this stuff away. Then I'll grab our breakfast. Do you need anything?"

"A big warm blanket, movies, and you."

Mariah smiles. "On it!"

I curl up on the couch and find *Mrs. Brown's Boys D'Movie* on Netflix. It's my favorite movie and a comedy. I feel like we need that. I settle in after I cue it up. Mariah grabs a large blanket and puts it in the dryer. She dishes up our breakfast and sets it on the coffee table for us with drinks. When she's finished, she grabs the blanket for us. We snuggle into each other and the blanket as I start the movie.

When we've finished breakfast, Mariah settles behind me and starts braiding my hair as she hums softly. When she finishes, she takes them all out and does it all over again. It's so soothing, I almost fall asleep against her.

Until she starts nibbling on my neck. Then, all of that sexual tension Matt built up rushes back full force and more. I truly crave them. All of them. I always want them. Now that I've had them, I want them so much more.

"Mariah…," I moan.

She nibbles on the other side of my neck. "Hmm…?"

"I might end up begging for release soon."

"Mmm…" She starts sucking on my neck as her hands snake under my shirt up to my tits. "That just might be the point. I have my orders, you know."

My eyes widen. That must be what Matt whispered in her ear. When she tugs on my nipples, I let my head fall back on her shoulder. My pussy is already pulsing, and she hasn't even touched me. I wiggle as she sends shivers through me. I grip her thigh and close my eyes. She nips my neck as she plays with my tits.

She never does one thing for long. The sensations are always different. She tugs on my nipples. She rubs my tits. She twists my nipples while she rubs my tits. It's always slow. She loves taking her time. I don't know if she knows just how wild she drives me.

I'm so focused on her mouth and hands, I don't realize that she's made her way with one of her hands into my sweats and down my panties until she's teasing my clit. I jerk into her, moaning, but Mariah is far stronger than she looks. She's holding me close to her with one arm. The jerk my mind thought would hurt me didn't hurt at all.

"Oh… my… God… Mariah," I pant. My clit is throbbing. My pussy pulses uncontrollably.

"I really love how you feel," she whispers in my ear. "I've always loved how wet you get." She keeps her thumb against my clit and rubs with the perfect amount of pressure as she thrusts two fingers deep into my pussy.

"Mariah!" I scream. My eyes roll back in my head. I clench so tight around her fingers that I don't know how she continues to move them.

But she does.

She thrusts at just the right speed, matching her rubbing of my clit to the same pace. I turn my head into her neck and arch the best I can into her fingers. She rubs my nipples with one hand and keeps thrusting with the other. She starts to alternate between rubbing and flicking my clit back and forth.

She kisses me so softly, and it's such a stark contrast to the sensations rocking my body, that I forget how to speak. I moan and whimper. My legs close around her hand, tightening my pussy even more.

"Come for me," she whispers as she kisses just below my ear. She knows I can't come without the command. I've only ever done it once, and it was because Matt and DJ weren't listening to my pleas. They kept teasing me until I lost control.

I scream again as wave after wave of pleasure overtakes me. One of the most powerful orgasms I've ever had strikes me. My pussy feels like it explodes. Hot liquid slides down my thighs and Mariah's hand. Mariah thrusts hard and deep and fast, making a complete mess of us both.

"Oh… Mmm…" I pant. "Oh…"

She thrusts slower and slower until I come down and fall limp against her. I moan quietly as she pulls her fingers out. I don't realize I've let my eyes close again until I feel her watching me. She's smiling softly as she sucks on her fingers.

"Mmm… So good." She nuzzles me.

I lower my lashes and blush shyly. "That's so hot."

She giggles and kisses me, letting me taste myself on her tongue. It makes me blush darker. I suck on her tongue. She tangles her fingers in my hair and deepens the kiss. I submit instantly and melt into her with a moan.

After we clean up and get settled again, Mariah puts one of her favorite movies on. *December*. I should have known. Mariah is such a history fanatic, and she loves everything to do with the second World War.

When Matt and DJ get home, we continue our movie night with grilled steaks for dinner and Mariah's maple bacon ice cream and fudge for dessert. We watch one of Matt's favorite movies, *White House Down*, and top off the perfect night with one of DJ's favorite movies, *Hobbs and Shaw*.

Mariah snuggles into DJ's lap and holds my hand as I cuddle into Matt's. The perfect night makes the morning a distant memory. All that matters is the four of us.

As I fall asleep with the three people who have become my world, I've never felt so safe, loved, or protected.

Home.

Chapter Eleven

☆ Matt ☆

(Three Weeks Later)

"You can't keep me on the desk," Sergeant Jackson growls at me from the chair in front of my desk.

"I have my orders. You almost killed Officer Sharpe by blatantly ignoring what was clearly in front of you on your clipboard. You knew those squads were up for repair. You put her in them anyway. I don't want to hear another fucking word. Go. Get out of my office."

He glares at me. "Just because you're fucking her doesn't give you the right to put me on a desk for a mistake."

I glare right back. "My relationship with her is none of your fucking business. What is my business is the safety of my officers. Putting you on the streets endangers all of them. Out. Now, Jackson." I glance up as Mariah stops outside my door. "I have other shit to do. Get out."

"I'm not fucking done with this. I'm sick and tired of you thinking you run the shop. You don't. Take me off the desk, or I'll go higher up the food chain."

"Go for it. I don't give a shit." I shrug.

He has another thing coming if he thinks we'll put him back on the streets when he's under investigation. But every day for the last three weeks since we put him there, it's been the same shit with him. He wants to be off the desk. He wants to be back on the streets.

Not a fucking chance.

Fuck. IA is sure taking their damn time with this.

"This isn't over," he says as threateningly as he can. He stands and places his hands on my desk. He leans over in an attempt to be menacing. I don't flinch. "I'm not going to let you walk all over me. I'm a good fucking cop. I deserve to be out there doing my damn job."

"Your job is behind a desk until you're told otherwise. You don't like it?" I point to my door. "There's the door. Don't let it hit you on the ass on your way out."

"Who do you think you're talking to? Are you fucking the Chief, too? Is that how you always get your way?"

I'm on my feet with my hand around his throat before I have a chance to stop myself. I pull him closer and smile devilishly at the gurgle. When he grabs my wrist, I smile wider and squeeze a little harder. His eyes bulge in surprise.

"One more fucking word about my sex life. I dare you," I say dangerously as I level him with my own glare. It would be so easy to rid the world of him once and for all.

"Matt," Mariah says quietly as she grabs my arm with one hand and puts the other against my chest. "Matt. Let him go. He's not worth it."

I look down at her, knowing she's right. I look back up at him. "Get the fuck back to your desk," I say with a vicious growl as I shove him backwards.

He looks at me wide-eyed, like he can't believe I dared put my hands on him. "You..."

"Get out!" I point to the door. He scrambles for the door rubbing his neck. I grip the edge of my desk as I watch him. He slams the door hard behind him.

"Sit, Matt. Please." Mariah softly rubs her hands up and down my chest and arm.

"I swear to fuck I'll kill him."

"Matt. Please." Mariah's voice is steady and calm. Her touch is gentle but firm as she pushes me into my chair. I watch her go to my door and lock it. She comes back to me and crawls in my lap.

I wrap my arms around her and hug her. "I've never been so close to snapping anyone's windpipe." I bury my face in her hair and let her scent soothe me.

"I know, but that's not going to get us anywhere. Or this investigation. We need to let IA do what they do. They're close to completing it, right?"

I hug her a little tighter. "They're done. We just got the report today. We have to have a meeting with the department heads. They aren't recommending the attempted murder charge that we asked for. They are recommending termination based on negligence. That's all."

"Well, you could go to the DA, right? The district attorney could make the decision to pursue that. Chief King could overrule the recommendation "

I sigh and pull away slightly but keep her in my arms. I love having either of my girls in my lap. It's comforting. "We don't have the evidence. DJ already went to the DA. He won't take the case. He can't prove anything."

She lets out a breath. "I thought that's what you were going to say."

I give her a soft smile and lean in. I kiss her softly. "Thank you for centering me again."

"You never need to thank me. It's the least I can do for all you do for me."

I smile and spend a few more minutes hugging my girl. The past three weeks have been incredible. We've spent a lot of time working on the dynamic of our relationship between the four of us. Though, it hasn't really taken a lot. Our relationship is truly effortless. It's one more reason I believe we're all meant to be together. Everything about us feels just the way it should. Being with all of them is my own Heaven.

I kiss Mariah's head softly. "You should get going to turnout."

She slumps slightly. "I object. I'm calling in sick."

I laugh. "Sick? What would your commanding officer say?"

She shrugs. "Who cares? My boyfriend is my commanding officer. And my other boyfriend is his, so…" She looks up at me teasingly.

I grin. "Oh, I see. You know, this is how it starts. I give you the day off now. All of the sudden you're taking advantage of my status as your boyfriend and also your Lieutenant. Before we know it, you're stealing money from drug busts and moving into the rich people's neighborhood."

She laughs her musical laugh that makes my dick hard instantaneously. "You forgot stealing the actual drugs and weapons. I'm going to own this city."

I groan when she wiggles against me. She knows exactly what she does. I gently push her up and swat her ass. "Go. I have a hard on to take care of. My girlfriend seems to think me walking into a meeting sporting one is a good thing."

Mariah's mouth drops. "That bitch. How evil."

I laugh at her deadpan look. "Give me a kiss and get out of here. I have shit to do. I can't do it if all I can think about is bending you over my desk."

"Jesus Christ, Lieutenant Chance. What would your girlfriend think?"

I laugh as she leans down and gives me the kiss I want. "Go bug your boyfriend." I swat her ass again.

She giggles. "Oh, DJ!" she calls in a teasing, sing-song voice as she unlocks my door.

I shake my head as I laugh. "You're trouble."

"I learned from the best."

"Hey. I'm an angel."

Mariah snorts out a laugh as I give her my most charming grin. "You are exactly the opposite. But I was talking about Lyric." She winks and closes my door behind her.

I laugh and shake my head. "That girl is going to be the death of me."

I glance at my clock and groan. IA requested a meeting with me, DJ, Chief King, and our Assistant Chiefs. They want to go over their report. Once that's finished, we're calling Sergeant Jackson in to give him the news. Whatever it is. My hope is a swift kick in the ass with orders to head for the unemployment line.

I grab my file and walk to the conference room. DJ is already sitting at the table. Both of our Internal Affairs officers are sitting on the other side of him. One of the Assistant Chiefs is sitting next to them. There are donuts and coffee sitting on the table. I take one and pour myself some coffee as I sit next to DJ.

"Should have known you'd grab the raspberry one," DJ says quietly as I settle.

"So nice of you to save it for me," I say just as quietly.

He chuckles and rubs his eyes. "Fuck, I want this done with. I don't think I've slept in a month."

"You've slept. Just not really well. With Lyric being as uncomfortable as she has been with her ribs and Mariah tossing and turning on top of the stress we're under, it's to be expected."

"I love our girls, but I'm going to start giving them sleeping pills pretty soon."

I chuckle. "The way we've all been sleeping, I'd say we all need them. You need a bigger bed if we're all going to keep sleeping together. That Queen ain't enough."

"Don't worry. I have an Alaskan King on its way."

I look over at him as I finish off my donut. "When did you order that?"

"Two days ago when Mariah and I fell out of the bed."

I smile at the thought. We were just waking up. DJ didn't realize how close he was to the edge of the bed. He turned over and lost his balance in his sleepy haze. Pulled Mariah with him. Mariah was so surprised at suddenly being on the floor, I don't think she even realized that DJ had been the one who took her with him.

"I can't say that wasn't funny." I lean back in my chair.

"Tell that to my dick. It hasn't recovered from Mariah's flailing foot."

I laugh as a couple other Captains and Lieutenants walk in followed by Chief King. DJ and I halt our conversation as everyone starts to settle. They grab their donuts and coffee. Some grumble at the early meeting, not totally sure why they're here to begin with.

"Who are we waiting on?" the Chief asks.

"Assistant Chief Drew, sir," I say.

"I'm here, Chief King!" Assistant Chief Drew says as she flies into the room. She quickly grabs a coffee and donut as she sits down. "I'm sorry I'm late. My eight year old decided today would be a good day to dress up as a dinosaur. Only dinosaurs don't wear clothes." Her eyes widen in horror. "Bill wasn't paying attention and almost let him out of the house to catch the bus like that. It was not a fun morning."

"I'm glad I never had kids," I say with a chuckle.

"Me, too," DJ agrees as he laughs and shakes his head. "Give me a teenager any day."

"They ain't all they're cracked up to be," one of the other Captains says. "My girl came home with a college boy who had piercings in places he shouldn't and was part of a gang. When I kicked him out, she decided she was going to run away."

"That was a fun case," the Lieutenant for our investigations department says. "We found her at his hideout and arrested seven of his friends. She was high as a kite. We saved her from a fate I don't think she had counted on."

I shake my head. "I'll never understand what young girls see in men like that."

"She learned her lesson. That's for sure. We had to put her in counseling for post-traumatic stress." He shakes his head.

"Sad it came to that," DJ says. "But maybe she'll learn from her mistakes and stay the fuck away from people like that."

"Damn right. I told her she's fucking grounded until she's fifty." We all laugh.

Chief King clears his throat. "Alright. We're here today because we have an issue with one of our Sergeants. Sergeant Jackson has been on desk duty for the past three weeks while IA has investigated him and some of his actions. He's specifically targeted two of our officers. We don't know why, but I'm hoping the investigation can shed some light."

"What exactly is going on?" another Lieutenant asks. "I was questioned about it, but no one could really say why."

Chief King nods. "Fair question. About a month before we put him on desk duty, Sergeant Jackson started ignoring our protocol when it came to squad assignment. As you all know, when our officers hit the streets, they are to check in with the Sergeant in the garage to grab their squad. The reason we do this is because some squads are deemed inoperable. We don't want our officers going out there with a squad that has brake problems or engine issues. It's dangerous for them. It's dangerous to the public. If their brakes go out, they could very well crash and cause an accident. People could be injured. Or worse."

DJ takes over when the Chief nods to him. "The problem was brought to my attention when I was meeting Officer Carter in the garage for a call out for our taskforce. When I got to the garage, she was being berated by Jackson. He was screaming at her about getting her ass on the streets. Something about not giving a shit about the fact that she had a call out or was meeting me. He told her to get out on the streets. They were short staffed. That morning, I had printed out a list of inoperable squads. Officer Carter's squad was inoperable. So was Officer Sharpe's. Jackson put Lyric into Lieutenant Chance's squad, as I had directed him to. I told him to put Mariah in mine. But that isn't what happened."

One of the IA guys stands and walks to a whiteboard he's already written on. "Jackson told Officer Carter that she would be driving squad eighty-two sixty-four that day. Squad eighty-two sixty four was on the inoperable list. The check engine light was on. It had been dying out. According to Officer Carter's statement, he'd told her it was fixed. The check engine light was on. It was a sensor."

"What the fuck?" a Captain says.

"It gets better," I growl. "Or worse. Whatever way you want to look at it."

"Much worse," our IA officer continues. "After Officer Carter took personal time, Sergeant Jackson set his sights on Officer Sharpe. Her squad was in the shop for about a week. After we got it back, he started giving it to other officers. He put Officer Sharpe into five different squads over the course of three weeks. All of them were on the inoperable list. According to Officer Sharpe's statement, she was put into a squad with front end issues, another with a starter issue, another that had a crack in the radiator and overheated on her on a traffic stop, and another squad with a head gasket issue. Finally, he put her in a squad that had a problem with the anti-lock brake system."

"Fuck me," a Lieutenant growls.

"Each of these squads were on an inoperable list given to him directly by Captain Rens," he continues. Everyone in the room is wearing the same angry expression that DJ and I are. "This particular squad was also on that list and was scheduled to be picked up and taken to the shop. Jackson told Sharpe the ABS light was on, but it was fine. She said it didn't cause her problems all day. Until a traffic stop. The woman she was pulling over panicked and slammed on her brakes when she saw she was being pulled over. Sharpe was forced to slam on her brakes to avoid hitting her. Sharpe ended up in a building when the brakes failed."

"That's what her injury leave was about," Chief King says. "We just told everyone that she was in an accident when the brakes in her squad failed. We didn't want it getting out what happened because we wanted IA to be able to do their job."

"I put Jackson on desk duty instead of Administrative Leave under the orders of Chief King," DJ says. "We didn't want him to be aware we were investigating him. With mine and Lieutenant Chance's involvement with Officer Sharpe and Officer Carter, we both pulled ourselves from any further dealings with him or his discipline. Any and all discipline came directly from the Chief."

"That hasn't stopped him from coming to my office every day for the past three weeks," I say. I wrestle with the thought of telling them I put my hands on the fucker. In the end, I decide to just be upfront. "Today, he came to my office and started complaining about being on desk duty. He kept telling me to put him back on the streets. He started bringing up my sexual relations with both Lyric and Mariah. The last straw was when he asked me if I was also fucking the Chief."

"For fuck's sake," Chief King scoffs.

I glance at him before exhaling a breath. "I would say that I regret to inform you I put my hands on the asshole, but I don't. I'll gladly take the write-up or the suspension, but I'm not going to tolerate him trying to bring my sex life or my girls into it. He's done enough to the both of them."

"What did you do, Chance?" Chief King asks with an almost chuckle as he shakes his head.

"I may or may not have choked him and shoved him out of my office." I grin, quite proud of myself. "He's lucky Mariah stopped the Marine in me from coming out. I didn't snap his windpipe."

The Chief laughs. "After we're done here, go home for the day. That's your discipline."

"That's not much of a punishment," DJ says, chuckling. "Lyric is still on leave."

"There's not a single person in this room who blames you for it," the other IA office says to me.

"Not a single fucking one," our other Assistant Chief says. "As far as I'm concerned, nothing happened."

Everyone in the room agrees. I don't know whether to be disappointed they're all covering for me or thankful. Truthfully, I should get a three day suspension at the very least, and charged with assault at the most. But I'm not going to complain. It's not like it's something I go around doing every day. Maybe if this was a constant thing, I'd be worried. When it comes to cops protecting other cops from danger, though, I can understand why they're all backing me. They probably all want to do the same thing.

"Anyway," our IA officer continues. "We found out through our investigation that he has a real problem with female officers. Ever since the accident with the female officer a few years ago. That's where it stems from. We think the reason he's gone after Mariah and Lyric specifically is the taskforce. He hates that it was created. He doesn't think it's necessary. He's been pretty outspoken about it taking away funds he believes could be better allocated to other things. Add on that they're female..."

The IA officers go through all of their evidence. When they are finished, Chief King sits quietly for a few minutes. I know he's wrestling with himself. He's been an advocate of charging Jackson with criminal neglect. The problem is he knows the DA won't take the case. He's already tried unsuccessfully.

Finally, he clears his throat. "I'll work on his termination. I'll pull him into my office with IA. I don't want Captain Rens or Lieutenant Chance involved in that part of it. Does anyone have anything they'd like to add? Any reason why I shouldn't terminate him?"

Everyone says no. I didn't believe anyone would disagree with a termination. None of us appreciate our officers being fucked around with. Especially when it's being done by another one. One who is in command is worse.

I follow DJ out. We don't talk until we reach his office. He closes the door behind us. He leans against it and lets out a long breath. I rub my temple and lean against the front of his desk.

DJ looks at me. "Finally, this nightmare ends."

"I still don't understand why he targeted them. Just the taskforce and because he has a problem with female cops?" I shake my head. It doesn't sit right with me. None of it does.

"Fuck, man. I don't know. A part of me doesn't care. As long as he isn't working here anymore."

"I know. It will put all of our minds at ease. I hate the idea that Mariah and Lyric felt unsafe in any manner."

He scrubs his hands down his face as he walks towards me. He puts his arms around my shoulder and kisses me so deeply, I can feel it in every part of my being. My hands automatically find his hips and pull him closer to deepen the kiss.

When he pulls away, I feel lightheaded. He smiles. "I needed that." He kisses me again. "Now head out. Before I decide to keep you in my office all day."

I laugh and reach down to give his dick a teasing squeeze. He groans and does the same to me in retaliation. I inhale sharply. DJ grins and kisses me as slowly as he's rubbing my dick. After a few moans and groans into each other's mouths, I force myself to pull away.

"You have work to do. And I'd better leave before the Chief has my ass."

He chuckles as I head for the door. We may tease each other, but I know as well as he does that if I don't leave now, I'll end up with his dick in my mouth. And he'll finish me off with my dick in his.

With Jackson the Jackass not hanging over us, though, I feel like we can all focus on what's important.

Each other.

Chapter Twelve

☆ *Mariah* ☆

I smile at the text from DJ saying we got the bastard. I can feel the tightness that has been in my chest for so long start to lift. It's like a giant weight has been removed from my heart. Not having Sergeant Jackson's antics hanging over me is like a breath of fresh air.

But most importantly, I'm glad he's not going to be around when Lyric returns. I feel like I can handle him a little better. Lyric is submissive by nature. She absolutely hates confrontation. She's been through a lot. I can't really blame her for hating when people yell at her. She avoids it at all costs.

I text DJ back quickly, telling him that I'm happy to hear that. He texts back right away, but I don't get the chance to read it when I get a call.

"Squad twelve."

I press the mic attached to my shoulder. "Go ahead."

"Disturbance. Caller says a man has been screaming obscenities at everyone walking by his house. He's sitting on the porch. She says she doesn't see any weapons."

I sigh. "Does the RP live in the area?"

"She lives across the street. She said he has people coming and going all through the night, but he's always been pretty quiet. This is something new. I sent you the address."

"10-4."

I pull the address up on my squad's laptop and sigh. I'm only a few blocks away, but I don't know how in the mood I am for someone who is probably hopped up on some psychedelic drug. As I turn onto the block, I look for the reporting party's house first to see what's going on before heading to confront the disturbing party.

It surprises me that this is actually a truly nice neighborhood. Usually, when we get calls about a disturbance where the person involved has activity all through the night, it means drugs. But as I step out of my squad, I can't see any other signs that drugs are the case. The guy isn't on his front porch. It doesn't look like he's even home.

"Squad twelve is two-three," I say into my mic, letting dispatch know that I've arrived at the location of my call.

"10-4."

I take a few more glances at the address of the disturbance while I walk up the path to the reporting party's house. I'm kind of on edge that everything is so quiet. Considering the type of call, I feel like the guy would still be out there.

Just as I'm about to knock, the door swings open to a wild-eyed looking woman. She looks over my shoulder at the house very nervously. Then she looks at my squad and hides behind her door so she's completely hidden by the door and me.

"I'm Officer Car -"

"Just come in. Please!" She waves me in and nervously chews her lip.

I take a quick glance inside her house and around the corner by her door before stepping inside. She very quickly closes the door and leans against it. She lets out a relieved sigh as she closes her eyes.

"Ma'am, I'm Officer Carter with Gainesville PD. Mind telling me what that was all about?" I say the words as soothingly as I can.

"Someone just went in there. He was driving an unmarked squad!"

I raise an eyebrow. "How do you know it was an unmarked squad?"

She shakes her head and wipes her eyes before looking at me. "Because the guy who got out was in a police uniform." She takes a breath. "I should start from the beginning."

"Yes. Please. That would be nice."

"I'm sorry. This has been a very hectic last few hours. So many things have happened. I just don't know where to even start."

"It's okay. Just start by taking a breath and telling me what led you to calling us." The fact that she's freaked out about an unmarked squad showing up but me not seeing it is troubling to me.

She takes a deep breath. "I came home from grocery shopping about two hours ago. He was just coming home. He was pissed. I mean truly pissed. He was cursing. He kicked the tire of his car. He was talking on his phone. He said he'd deal with it. He saw me looking. I turned away quickly, but he started to scream at me. He started coming across the street. I ran inside with my grocery bags. I thought he was going to get to me before I opened the door, but he stopped in the middle of the street."

I nod and rest my arms on my gun and taser. "Did he come any closer than that? Did he pound on your door? Anything?"

She shakes her head. "No. No ma'am. He just screamed from the middle of the street at me."

"What was he saying?"

"That I should mind my own business. That it's not polite to listen in on private conversations. He called me a bitch and stupid and a slut. He told me he was going to kick my ass if I ever walked out of the house. I didn't call the police right away because he went away. He went inside his house. I took a few minutes to calm down. I put my groceries away. The next thing I hear is him screaming again. He was sitting on his porch. I looked out the window very cautiously. I didn't want him to see me." She looks down.

"And then what happened, Ms. Lamport?"

"He screamed at three other people from his porch. I finally called when he yelled at a little kid who was walking with her dog. I was on the phone with the police while I was yelling at him to leave that little girl alone. She ran away. She's safe. He directed his attention back to me. The police said someone was on the way and to go back inside and lock the door. I did. While I was waiting for you, I saw a black car come up with a spotlight on the side. I thought it was you. I was watching. The guy was in uniform. He got out. He looked around. They both looked at my house. They didn't see me."

"Are you sure they didn't see you?"

She nods. "Yes, ma'am. I was watching through the peephole in my door. The officer was talking to him. Then he parked his car in the garage."

I raise an eyebrow. "Who parked the car in the garage?"

"The cop. He parked his car in the neighbor's garage."

I furrow my brows and cross my arms over my chest. Something about this entire thing doesn't seem right to me. I reach for my mic, but think better of it. I don't like the fact that there is seemingly a cop at this guy's house. He could have a radio and be listening.

"Did you see if the cop left?"

"No, ma'am. He didn't. He's still there."

I reach for my cell phone with a nod. I realize I left it in my car. I sigh. "Can I use your phone?"

"Of course. It's right over here." She leads me to the phone and walks over to her window. She peeks out of the curtains that she's closed and stays hidden. I quickly dial Matt's office phone. When he doesn't answer, I dial DJ on his department cellphone and wait for him to answer.

"Captain Rens," he says into the receiver.

"DJ? It's Mariah," I say quietly. "Is Matt busy? I have a problem."

"I texted you. Matt was sent home for the day for choking Sergeant Jackson. What's going on?"

I sigh. "I was afraid he'd get in trouble for that."

"He's not. He was just sent home. What's going on? What's the problem? And why are you calling me from a random number?"

I rub my temple. "I was sent to a disturbance. The phone is the RP's. I left my cell in the car. Can you look up the call I'm on?"

"Yeah. I'll do it now. What happened?"

"Well, my RP said in the initial call that the guy has people coming and going all through the night. My initial gut reaction is drug dealer, and he's tripping. But when I got here, it looks like no one is home. I went to the RP first because there was nothing that looked to need immediate intervention." I pause and take a deep breath as I lower my voice. "DJ, she said a cop showed up. In uniform. They talked outside. The cop put his car in the garage of this house. And not just that. This neighborhood is a nice neighborhood. I'm talking like HOA type of housing. Everything is immaculate. It doesn't make sense."

"Fuck…"

His tone makes my heart quicken in alarm. "What?"

"Don't fucking do anything until I get there. Do you understand me?"

I blink. "Y-Yes, but what am I missing?"

"No calls on the radio. Nothing. Sit tight right where you are."

"O-Okay. DJ what's -" I'm cut off when he hangs up. I stare at the receiver in disbelief before replacing it in its cradle.

"Was that your boss?"

"Yeah. Yeah. Um… yeah." I take a breath to steady myself before turning to her. A cop always has to portray professionalism. Confidence. I have the professionalism in spades. The confidence, though, I am currently lacking. So, I fake it.

"What did he say?"

"Honestly? He's coming here. I think he's picking up on something that I'm not. So we're going to observe." I walk to the other side of her window and peek out. "What else can you tell me about him?"

"Well, he's really quiet. Or at least he had been. For many, many years. He always put up super fun and creative decorations during all of the holidays. But over the last couple of years, he's been doing less and less. I rarely see him leave the house, but I always see him return."

"When does he return?" I hate how quiet everything is. It makes me uneasy. Coupled with DJ's tone, and I'm more on edge than I've been with most any call I've been on in my career.

"He always gets home between four and five in the afternoon."

My stomach clenches, but I don't know why. "What about the nighttime activity?"

"Oh, that's new. That just happened…" She trails off when I get a call.

"Squad twelve."

I feel like the panic is rising. DJ said no radio contact. But I know if I don't answer, they'll send a squad to check on me. I take a breath. "Go ahead."

"Status check."

I let out a relieved breath and nod. "Code four."

"10-4."

I glance over at Ms. Lamport. "Sorry. You were saying?"

"Actually, it started happening about the same time he started becoming a shut-in. And it's so weird. I wake up during the night to go to the bathroom. All hours. My bedroom is just above us. It faces his house, too. It doesn't matter what time I'm up. There is always someone arriving at his house or leaving it. All hours."

"Step back from the window," I order as I step back myself.

"Why?" She steps away from the window. I'm thankful she does what I say

"I saw the curtain move. I didn't get a good look at the person, but I caught a glimpse of a badge and his gun. It was definitely a cop." I cross to the phone again and call DJ on his cell.

"I'm almost there," he says gruffly.

"Wait. Just wait a second. Don't turn down the street."

"Mariah, I'm not leaving you there on your own."

"DJ. Please. Just trust me. Wait." I look at Ms. Lamport. "Do you have a back entrance?"

"He can park in the alley and come in the backdoor, but I don't have a driveway back there."

I nod. "Park in the back of my RP's address. Come in the backdoor. Just trust me."

"You know I trust you. I'm turning down the alley now."

"Okay." I hang up. "Can you show me to the back?"

"Of course." She leads me through her house to her kitchen.

She opens the back door as DJ is crossing her yard. I can't help but be thankful that he decided not to wear his uniform today. Usually, he does when he has to meet with higher up commanding officers. Today, he's decided on black slacks and a shirt with a tie. His gun is secured in his shoulder holster. His badge is fastened to his belt. He doesn't drive a marked squad, so he's not drawing any attention to us.

DJ's eyes meet mine as he shakes Ms. Lamport's hand. "Ms. Lamport. I'm Captain DJ Rens. Looks like we're in some kind of a pickle."

"You have no idea," she says as she shakes his hand and lets him in.

He closes the door behind him. "So, tell me what's going on?"

I lead him back to the front room. "A lot. First and foremost, there's definitely a cop over there. I just saw him through the window. But other than that? I don't know. This stuff doesn't make sense to me. I think we need to set up surveillance."

DJ nods. "Start from the beginning."

"Well, I told you how I ended up here. After we hung up, Ms. Lamport said that there was a lot of activity going on. All hours of the night. She gets up to go to the bathroom. Her bedroom faces his house. He's got people coming and going all the time. She said that the cop that's over there right now parked his car in the garage."

DJ looks at Ms. Lamport. "When did all of this start happening today? The disturbance?"

"It was about two hours ago. I was bringing groceries home. He arrived just about the same time I did. He was talking on the phone. Yelling. He kicked his tire. He said something about him taking care of it. I don't know what. He saw me looking. He started yelling at me. He came towards me. He was yelling at me, but he stopped halfway across the street. He never came any closer. He just yelled at me."

"He told her to mind her own business. He said if she ever comes out of her house, he'll kick her ass. But he never came closer than halfway across the street."

"He went inside for a little while. But then he came back out. He started yelling at people. I called the police when he started in on a little girl walking her dog. I opened my door and told him to leave her alone. He freaked out at me again. I closed the door when the girl ran away. I was on the phone with the police."

I cross my arms over my chest. "As she was waiting for me, an unmarked squad showed up."

DJ raises an eyebrow. "How did you know it was a squad?"

"There was a spotlight on the driver's side," Ms. Lamport says. I know police do auctions so that may not have been the deciding factor. "But it was the uniformed cop that came out of the squad that confirmed it."

I bite my lip and smile because I can hear the humor in her voice. Knowing DJ as well as I've come to, I know that, while he enjoys humor, he doesn't enjoy when anyone comes off condescending like she just did. But I think it's funny when people get under his skin just a little bit.

DJ shakes his head slightly at me when he sees my reaction. He chuckles. "Okay, Ms. Lamport. What else can you tell me?"

"Well, this wasn't a thing until a couple of years ago. About the time he started decorating less and less for the holidays was about the time that the activity started at his house."

DJ nods. "Can you tell me if he had any family?"

Ms. Lamport's eyes widen. "Actually, now that I think about it, he did. He had a little girl and a pretty young wife. But I stopped seeing them around the time his behavior changed. He never said anything about what happened. I honestly didn't ask. We've never been really close. I figured it was a divorce."

I kick myself for not asking that. DJ crosses his arms over his chest. "Ms. Lamport, do you happen to know his first and last name?"

"I don't know his last name. And for some reason, he's never put it on his mailbox. But his first name is Isaac."

"Thank you, Ms. Lamport," DJ says. "We're going to set up surveillance. If you see anything else suspicious, note it down for us. Don't interact with him. Don't try to get any pictures. Don't let him see you watching him. Just go about your usual business. If you wake up in the middle of the night and see someone coming or going, note it down. We'll be checking in with you."

She nods and breathes a sigh of relief. "Thank you, Captain Rens." She shakes his hand and turns to me. "And thank you, Officer Carter."

"You're welcome," I say with what I hope is a sweet smile and not the confused one I really want to show.

DJ starts to guide me out the backdoor. He turns when we're just about to leave. "One more question."

"Sure, Captain."

"The officer who showed up. Have you ever seen him before?"

"Oh. No. Actually, I haven't. It's concerning to me. It set me a little uneasy. It wasn't until Officer Carter showed up that I decided all of Gainesville PD wasn't involved in whatever he has going on."

DJ smiles a charming smile. "I assure you, ma'am," he drawls. I shiver. "I want to get to the bottom of this as much as you do. I'll be in touch." He guides me quickly to his squad. "Get in."

"My squad is out front."

"Mariah." His tone is dominant enough to make me listen and stop questioning.

I climb in the passenger seat. DJ says nothing as he turns the vehicle on and starts to slowly drive down the alley. I watch him both curiously and beyond confused. I'm still unsure what he isn't telling me. All I know is that it was something that had to have freaked him out.

He turns down the block and slowly drives down the street. He turns on the street my squad is parked and stops at the end of the block. He hasn't looked at me. I'm not convinced he's even breathing until he lets out a long breath.

"Tell me everything that throws you off about this." He keeps his eyes straight ahead.

"Uh… Everything. Like how she doesn't know his last name, but he's apparently lived in the area for years. At least long enough that when his habits changed, she noticed. How does she not know what happened to his family? Who is the cop? What is going on? Why the sudden change? What happened to his family? Who is he?"

DJ takes a deep breath. "His family was killed in a car accident. It really fucked him up. He was off work for almost three months. We were all pretty surprised he even came back. He was the one driving the car. He was the only survivor."

I shake my head trying to follow. How does he know that? "Wait. We were all pretty surprised? That would mean…" I look out the window towards the house. That sick and uneasy feeling rises again as realization hits.

DJ just nods. "Isaac. Recognize the name?"

I shake my head slowly. "Should… I?" I feel like I should, but I don't.

"Isaac Jackson, baby."

"Oh… my God," I breathe. "Sergeant. Sergeant Isaac Jackson." I tangle my fingers in my hair and shakily lean against the window. "That would mean…"

DJ nods again. "That would mean this was all a trap."

Chapter Thirteen

☆ DJ ☆

I shakily run my fingers through Mariah's hair and lean over. I kiss her deeply, thankful as all hell she's fucking alive. As soon as I saw the address of the call, I knew. I knew exactly what was going on.

We'd just fired Isaac Jackson a couple of hours before Mariah had called. I'd had a few things that I needed to do administratively after the termination. Namely, replacing the fucker on all of my staff schedules. I may not have been involved in the termination, but I still have a job to do replacing him with my staff.

I'd heard he threw a fucking fit like a three-year old who had a sucker taken away. I was pretty upset I didn't get to see his ass being escorted out the door after he was forced to turn in his shield, uniform, and all his department issued gear.

Unfortunately, we buy a lot of our own stuff. Handcuffs, mase, batons, flashlights, bullets, and our guns. Which means he still has all of that stuff. Given what I know about him, the fact that he has guns and any of that other equipment puts me in a world of unease.

Fear even.

"What else do you know about him?" Mariah asks quietly. She nuzzles me and rests her head on my shoulder as we both hug each other. I know she understands I need this. I'm sure after she realized what just happened, she needs it just as much.

"That's all. When he came back, he was a changed man. He had a few complaints. A few write-ups for being an asshole. Mostly to our female cops. But it was nothing like you and Lyric. His bark had always been worse than his bite. This is such a huge fucking change. But when I saw that address, baby, I almost stopped breathing. He knows you work in his district."

"Why didn't he come after me when I first arrived?"

"I don't know." I slowly pull away. "I don't have any idea, Rih. But I don't trust it."

"Squad four."

We both jump at the sound of dispatch on the radio. I take my mic. "Go ahead."

"I have a phone call for you. Can I send it to your squad?"

I raise an eyebrow and look at Mariah a little uncomfortably. Dispatch doesn't often send calls to my squad. "Yeah. Sure." Seconds later, my squad cell phone rings. Both of our eyes widen when we see the number. I put it on speaker. "Ms. Lamport?"

"Captain Rens! Thank God. I ran to the back of the house as quickly as I could and tried to flag you down. I didn't see you come back to Officer Carter's squad."

I put my squad in gear and start slowly rolling down the street. "We're at the end of the block. We're just discussing our next course of action. Is something wrong?"

"I went back to my window. I wanted to make sure that Officer Carter got to her squad okay. I saw that cop across the street!"

"Okay. It's okay, Ms. Lamport. Is he leaving?" I near Mariah's squad from the opposite direction of what she's parked. I watch her smile when she realizes what I'm doing. I'm effectively using my squad to block her from Isaac's house as she gets into her squad by making sure that when she gets out of my squad, she gets out on the side of Ms. Lamport's home.

"Captain Rens, stop! You don't understand!"

I glance at Mariah as I stop just in front of her squad. "Ms. Lamport, what's going on?"

She's starting to hyperventilate. "He has a gun pointed right at you!"

No sooner do the words leave her lips, shots ring out. Mariah screams as glass shatters. I cover my head and push Mariah down towards my lap as I duck. The driver's side window shatters around me. The rate the bullets are flying is too fast to be a shotgun or a semi-automatic. This fucker has a fucking automatic rifle.

I slam my squad into gear and peel out. I race down the street with my head barely up enough to see where I'm going. I know full well he can still hit my squad even though I'm not in front of his house anymore.

I hear Ms. Lamport scream. "He's shooting at my house!"

I whip the squad around the corner. I keep Mariah down. She's screaming and crying as she hyperventilates. "Ms. Lamport, I'm coming! Back of the house! Don't stop for anything! Just run!"

"He's running across the street!"

"Run!" I whip into the alley, fishtailing around the corner and slam on the gas. I hear the phone clattering and Ms. Lamport screaming. I can hear more shooting. "Mariah, you need to help me out. Okay?" I tug gently on her hair. "You have to hold on for me and cover me so I can get Ms. Lamport."

She shakily nods as she reaches for her gun. She slides down onto the floor and hits the button so her window comes down. I skid to a stop as she braces herself. She pokes her head up just far enough so she can see. I jump out, staying low.

Ms. Lamport comes flying out of the house at full speed, screaming. She runs towards me. "He's in there! He came through the shattered window!"

I stay as low as I can, using my squad for cover. "Don't stop running!" I yell. I see Isaac Jackson reach the door of the house. My heart stops when he takes a knee and aims. I don't have a clear shot at him. Not with Ms. Lamport running towards me.

Before I can tell Ms. Lamport to get down, Mariah shoots towards the house. One of her shots hits Isaac somewhere. I can't tell where, but he falls backwards before catching himself and dropping his rifle. I pray like fuck that when I see him reaching up to his left side that he's reaching for his heart.

I catch the glimpse of someone else. While I can't tell who it is, the sun shines off something shiny and metal on his left side, just above his heart. There's no doubt that whoever that is, he's a fucking cop.

When Ms. Lamport gets to me, I grab her arm and pull her behind the SUV. I drag her to the back of the SUV and open the backdoor for her. I take the sweater she has tied around her waist and use it to quickly brush the seat off so she isn't sitting on broken glass. She doesn't hesitate to get in as fast as she can.

"Get down," I command. She does. I slam the door and jump in the driver's seat. Staying low, I slam the SUV into gear and drive as swiftly as I can. I whip onto the street and speed away in the opposite direction of Issac's.

"Holy fuck...," Mariah whispers from the floor.

"Call this in, Rih. I need to watch for anyone following."

She presses the mic on her shoulder. "Squad tw-twelve to dispatch."

"Go ahead."

"Sh-shots fired. At my location. Two suspects. First suspect is Is-Isaac Jackson. Former Gainesville PD Sergeant. Terminated today. Second suspect is un-unknown. Uniformed police officer. Unknown if he's from our department. Unmarked sq-squad parked in Jackson's garage. Suspects fi-fired on myself and Captain Rens. Suspects entered RP's home through a window they sh-shot out. Fired on h-her as well." She looks up at me.

"We're going to the station with Ms. Lamport," I say, knowing what she's going to ask.

"Myself and Captain Rens are en route to HQ with RP. Un-unknown where suspects are. Jackson was shot in the shoulder."

I glance in the mirror at Ms. Lamport. She's trembling. I can't blame her. It's not every day a person gets shot at. It's also not every day that I walk away from a situation like that. I know how much shit I'm going to take for it. A cop doesn't walk away from a situation where lives are in danger.

When I'm satisfied we aren't being followed, I take my radio. "Squad four to radio. I want SWAT on location to clear my RP's and Isaac Jackson's home." I take a breath. No cop wants to say what I'm about to. "Be aware we're after an ex-cop and another person who might be one of our own."

"10-4."

"Matt is SWAT…," Mariah sniffles from the floor as she looks up at me.

"He won't get called out. He's technically on a suspension." My cell phone rings. I put it on speaker and answer. "Rens."

"What the fuck is going on, Cap? I heard the call. Sergeant Jackson's house?"

I take a breath and rub my temple. Blake Erickson is our third in command. He's a Sergeant and in charge if me or Matt aren't there. We won't be. Given our history with the fucker, it's a conflict of interest. Much to my dismay. He shot at my girl and damn near took out a woman who might be around ten years my senior. I'd love to be the one to take the shot.

"You're in command, Erickson. Sergeant Jackson was just fired today. Long story short, he was fucking around with Sharpe's and Carter's lives. He was behind Lyric's accident. Put her in several squads that were on the inoperable list. He's been messing around with Carter for a while."

"Fuck. I'm sorry, man."

I just nod. Blake is one of the few who know about my relationship with both girls and Matt. "Mariah was called to a disturbance. She didn't know his address. Name of the person of interest was never given in the call. She was smart and went to talk to the RP first. She called me when things weren't adding up. She wanted to set up surveillance. She thought it was a drug house, but it was in a neighborhood you wouldn't ever see that shit in. She told me to look up the call. I had Jackson's file in front of me because I was dealing with paperwork and shit. As soon as I saw where she was sent, I fucking knew."

"He was setting her up."

"That's what I think. I don't know why they didn't take their shot when she showed up."

"They?"

"Yep. There's a second cop involved. RP saw him show up. Parked his car in Jackson's garage. We haven't been able to identify him. When we left, we went out the back. I didn't trust the idea of sending Mariah out front to her squad. I had parked in the back on Mariah's orders. I parked at the end of the block after we left to tell her what was going on before I drove her to her squad. I thought I could block her from his house when I dropped her off at her squad."

"I'm assuming that didn't work out."

"Fuck no. RP called us. Told us she saw him with a gun pointing at us. No sooner did she say the words, all hell broke loose. They have an automatic weapon. My squad is shot up. I know I'll answer for making the decision to leave the scene, but we were not equipped to go up against that. I may have stayed, but our RP was still on the phone. She was screaming they were going for her. They shot out her window. Entered her house."

"Shit."

"I circled around and got her from the back of her house. Jackson was at the backdoor. They chased her from the inside. She got out. He was aiming right for her. Mariah got a shot off. Hit Jackson in the shoulder. I think. Fuck of a shot from twenty-five yards."

"I'd say. Maybe we should recruit her to SWAT."

I chuckle and glance down at her as I pull into the garage. She's curled into herself. "I don't think she'd like that very much. Anyway. The cop showed up behind him. I couldn't see his face. He pulled Jackson back. I don't know if they're still there."

"Doubt it. I'm sure they ran. Especially if he knows you know who he is. I'm sure the other cop isn't sure if you know who he is or not, but I doubt he'd take a chance."

"If he was in uniform, he might have a radio."

"He doesn't," Ms. Lamport says.

I glance in the mirror as I park. "He doesn't?"

She shakes her head and wipes her eyes. "No, sir. I got a very clear view of him. He was wearing all of the equipment that Officer Carter is, but he didn't have a radio on his belt or the thing that comes up on her uniform." She hugs herself.

I nod. "Okay."

"I'm operating like he does. He might have one in his squad. If they left, chances are they took the squad. Less conspicuous."

"Just get over there. Take the team. Clear the area. Operate like he's there."

"On it, boss. What do you want me to say to any commanding officers who come to me about you leaving?"

"Tell them I left because I had their targets with me. My fucking job is to save lives. I'm not going to get into a shootout in the middle of the goddamn neighborhood if I think I can stop it by removing the targets."

"Yes, sir. I mobilized some officers already to set up a perimeter. I'm just arriving on location."

"Command is yours. Keep me updated."

"You got it." He hangs up.

I take a second to compose myself before looking down at Mariah. She's still on the floor. "You can get up, sweet girl. We're at HQ."

She takes a deep breath and uncurls herself as she climbs up to the seat. She shakily reaches for the door handle and opens it. I open mine and get out. I close it slowly and use the extra time to school my composure before opening the backdoor for Ms. Lamport. I help her out as I watch Mariah. Both are shaking.

Mariah hugs herself as she silently leads us all into the station. Ms. Lamport is holding my arm like she's going to fall over. While I feel bad for her and care for her, Mariah is my concern. She's never been shot at before. At least for real. Training is far different then real life. Real bullets. Real consequences. I know she's struggling with this.

Mariah stops outside one of our interview rooms closest to my office and looks up at me. She's putting on a brave face, but I can see the real emotions she's shoving down for the sake of Ms. Lamport. I lead Ms. Lamport into the room. Mariah helps her settle and quietly grabs a statement form and pen. She sets it on the table.

"Can I get you anything to drink?" I ask her. "We have coffee. I can't promise it's good. I think I have some instant cappuccino in my office."

"That sounds nice," she whispers. Mariah quietly goes to make it.

"Can I call anyone for you?"

She shakes her head and shivers. It's then I remember her sweater. It's chilly in here. The air conditioner never works properly, but I can see the goosebumps forming on her bare arms as she rubs them.

"I don't have any family here. No friends I can depend on in this situation. What would I say?" She gives me a sarcastic smile. "Hey there. I was shot at. I need to stay with you."

"If there's anyone you think would be willing to and understanding, that's exactly what I'd say."

"No. Thank you, Captain. I'll just go to a hotel."

"Ms. Lamport, with all due respect, you have no clothes. No purse. I can't allow you to go back to your house. And I won't let you be alone. You're obviously a target. I won't put you in a hotel unless it's a last resort. Given how much trouble I'm about to be in, I highly doubt I'll get department authorization to put you in a hotel on our dime with a twenty-four hour watch. And even if I did, I can't be sure I can trust everyone. I'd have to pull one of my team members, and I know they won't authorize that. So we have two choices. We call someone you trust that I can place you with. Somewhere nowhere near your home. Or I take you home with me and you stay with me, Mariah, and our other boyfriend and girlfriend. It's your call."

"Rens!" a deep, booming voice yells.

I wince slightly as Mariah comes back into the room. "Make your decision, Ms. Lamport." I turn to Mariah. "Get her my hoodie out of my office. She's cold. And help her with her statement. Make sure she's as comfortable as you can make her." I kiss the top of her head as I leave the room. I walk straight into Chief King.

He narrows his eyes and points to my office. "Go."

I hold his gaze a second before sighing and closing the door to the interview room. I lead him to my office and close the door behind us both as Mariah sneaks by and walks back to the interview room with my hoodie.

I don't say a word. I just sit down behind my desk and wait. Chief King watches me with his arms folded over his chest. Finally, he sits. He watches me for several moments. But I still don't say anything.

He sighs. "What the fuck were you thinking? You left two armed gunmen at the scene of a crime."

"My job is to save lives. I saved three lives today. Mariah's. Ms. Lamports. And mine."

"You put many more lives in danger by leaving."

"Did I?" I lean back in my chair as he stares at me incredulously. "I removed the targets. Remove the targets. Remove the threat."

"Who the fuck taught you that? Is that in our training curriculum? Because I don't think so."

"It was my call. They had an automatic weapon. I had an AR-15. I had one cop in the midst of a panic attack she hasn't come out of. I had an RP in the middle of fucking shootout. I was in a quiet neighborhood where

I didn't know if people were home. I didn't know how many possible victims I could have had if any stray bullets had gone through a window. I didn't know if anyone would be stupid and come outside to see what the commotion was about. I decided to call off the gunfight. That was my call. And it's a call I made as a commanding officer based on the information I had in front of me. It's a call I stand by and would make again. It's no different to me than calling off a high speed chase to save lives."

He sighs. "You left two armed suspects in a neighborhood, DJ. I can't let this slide."

"I don't expect you to. I'll take the punishment. I don't care. But I made the call I did to protect everyone in that area. It was dangerous. It could have gotten far more out of control. If I hadn't been on the phone with that woman, Chief, if she hadn't called to warn us, I don't know what would have happened. You could have three dead bodies. I moved less than a second before the first shot."

He scrubs his hand down his face. "I have to suspend you, DJ. I don't have a choice. You went so far beyond protocol. I can't defend that."

I shake my head and lean forward. I fold my hands on my desk. "Then you need to suspend Mariah, too. She discharged her weapon and hit Jackson. I think in the shoulder. Can't be sure."

"Fucking hell, DJ." He sighs. "I can't lose four of my best fucking cops. Lyric being out with injury. You. Her. Matt. Christ. This is a mess."

"Yep. We also have another officer who is working with Jackson. Don't know who, but he's driving an unmarked squad."

"Do you have any fucking good news for me?"

"Yeah. We survived. As far as I know, no dead bodies. Including Isaac Jackson. Much to my dismay." I stand. "You going to let me do my job?" I take off my badge and put it on my desk. "Or do you want my shield?" Part of me wants him to say I'm suspended. It means I can go home and protect my family as well as the innocent bystander put in the way of a sick game. The other part of me wants to finish this.

Chief King sighs. "Fine. You stay on. I'll go to bat for you because I agree with your actions. I can't say others will."

"Fair." It feels good to have him on my side.

"But Mariah gives her statement and leaves. Whether she likes it or not. I'm suspending her under the guise of her discharging weapon.

Department protocol. But between us, it's for her own fucking good. My way of protecting her. This is out of control."

"I agree." I fasten my badge back to my belt. "I want Matt suspended for the incident with Jackson."

He gives me a confused look. "He already technically is."

I shake my head. "If Lyric and Mariah are going to be home, they'll be alone. If you aren't suspending me, then we're suspending Matt. It stays out of his jacket, but I want someone with them."

He nods in understanding. "If that's what you want."

"It's what I want. I don't want my family alone. And I have a feeling we'll be having Ms. Lamport as a guest until this is over. She doesn't have family here, and we can't afford round the clock surveillance and a hotel."

"As much as I hate to agree, you're right." He stands. "Figure out who we're missing that's driving an unmarked car today."

"Yes, sir."

"Keep me updated on what's going on with this, Rens."

"You got it."

He nods as he leaves. I let out a breath before walking to the interview room to grab Mariah. I don't say anything as I lead her back to my office, but when I close the door, I wrap her in my arms. For the first time, she lets loose and cries. She collapses in my arms as she hangs onto me for all she's worth.

"God, DJ…"

I bury my face in her hair and hug her as tightly and close as I can. "I know, baby. Fuck, I'm never letting you go again."

Chapter Fourteen

☆ Lyric ☆

"Oh… God, Matt," I moan into Matt's neck as I grip his shoulders.

He plunges his dick into me again and again as he holds me against the wall. "Fuck, beautiful. I needed this."

I grip his shoulders and tighten my legs around his waist to gain more leverage. He grips my ass tighter and lifts me before dropping me back onto his dick as he thrusts into me hard. My pussy clenches around him with each thrust, making me tighter for him. I learned rather quickly that he loves when I do it. It drives him closer and closer to the edge far quicker than it would if I didn't. I only do it when I need release, and he's not there yet.

Just as I need him to, his dick jerks inside me, and he moans. He drives into me faster until my pussy is pulsing uncontrollably around him. My eyes roll back in my head. I scratch across his back and bite his shoulder with a whimper. He slaps my ass and nips my neck.

"Matt, please!"

He thickens inside me and grunts before he plunges as deep as he can and holds himself. "Please?"

"Please!" I'm so close. The ledge is within my grasp.

Matt doesn't move. He kisses my neck slowly. "Please what? Please kiss you?" He pulls his dick all the way out of me as he kisses me hard. He slams it back in, sending shockwaves through my body.

I scream into his mouth, but can't say anything. My thighs tremble. Matt pulls out again and slams himself hard back into me. He slowly pulls away from the kiss. I'm throbbing around him. Pulsing erratically.

"Oh God! Please, Matt! Please let me come for you. I want to come for you!" I clench my legs even tighter as I thrust myself over him. "Matt! Please!" I throw my head back. I'm losing grip on myself. There's no way I can hold on much longer.

He gives me a wicked smile. "Good girl. I love when you ask so nicely. Come, sweet girl. Come for me."

The command is all it takes. But when he starts giving me hard, deep, fast thrusts once more, I'm gone. I sail into an alternate universe. An earthquake starts in my clit and travels through my pussy. My whole body convulses as I come hard for him, soaking his dick and my thighs.

"Matt!" I scream. He keeps thrusting as I come. His lips are against my neck when he moans. The thrusts that don't slow bring me closer and closer to a powerful aftershock. The tremors get stronger and stronger.

Finally, Matt buries himself once again and comes so hard I feel like it surges throughout my veins. I nearly blackout as I collapse against him and spasm as a second release hits me. I pant and try to hold onto him, but I feel like my limbs are getting weaker and weaker as the seconds pass.

Matt, being as intuitive as he is, feels it. He holds me tighter and walks us both to the couch. Still buried inside me, he lays down on his back. He rubs his hands up and down my back and kisses my neck up to my cheek and to my lips.

He pushes my hair behind my ear as I continue to tremble. "Let go, baby. It's okay. I got you."

I bury my face in his neck and do exactly that. My body relaxes fully. I feel like I melt into him. My limbs feel like jelly. I let myself pant to catch my breath. I breathe him in and allow myself to be lulled by the steady rhythm of his heart.

Several moments later, when I come back to myself, I shiver. Matt's arms tighten around me as he slowly lets himself slide out of me.

The sweat from our three rounds of lovemaking has begun to dry. It's making me slightly cold.

I reluctantly start to push myself up as I look towards the window. "It's really getting dark." The entire reason for the marathon sex slams into me. "I'm really worried."

Matt sits up slowly and shifts us so I'm sitting in his lap. "Honestly, so am I. Want me to try calling Mariah again? Or DJ?"

"They haven't responded to our repeated calls or messages." I look at my phone sadly.

Matt kisses me. "Don't worry, baby. I'm sure there's a reason."

DJ and Mariah were supposed to be home over four hours ago. But the longer it takes them to come back, the more worried I become. I keep saying that maybe they're tied up on a call, but I wish one of them would at least text. My mind has gone in hundreds of different directions. None of them are good.

I sigh and reach from my phone just as it rings. My eyes widen. "Mariah? Where are you?"

"Put it on speaker," Matt whispers. I do and hold it so we can both hear her.

Mariah sniffles. "It's... been a truly bad day. It's a lot to explain on the phone."

"Well, try, baby. Lyric and I are worried as fuck about you both."

"Really, Rih. It's been like four hours since you both were supposed to be home." I rub my chest. I know something isn't right. I can feel it.

"Well, long story short. We have another bad cop. We don't know who he is. But he was with Jackson today on a call I was on that led to me calling DJ because something didn't add up. Then DJ showed up to my RP's house. Then we both got shot at. So..., like I said. Long day. Too much to explain over the phone."

I can feel the tears sting my eyes. "Mariah! What? You can't leave it like that!"

She sniffles again. "Please, Lyric. We'll explain when we're home. Can you please order something for dinner? We'll be having a guest. I need one of you to please grab a pair of sweats and a hoodie from my drawer for her. We'll be there soon."

I look up at Matt frantically, willing him to make her explain. He nods. "Mariah. That's not how this is going down. Talk to us. What the fuck happened?"

She sighs. "Matt, please. I haven't had a second to breathe. I just got my phone back. I fought a panic attack off on my own because DJ had been called in more directions than I even really know. Please just… Just let us get home. I can't… I can't explain this myself." She chokes on a sob. "Please."

Her sob makes my heart hurt and my chest constrict. "Okay…," I whisper as Matt puts an arm around me and pulls me close.

"Okay, baby. Okay. We'll take care of it. Just get home safe, please." Matt kisses the top of my head.

"Thank you," she whispers. "I love you both. So much." She hangs up before either of us have a chance to say anything. I feel my throat tighten. Matt inhales sharply.

None of us have said those words before. I've felt it for a long time. I never really believed that anyone could fall in love so quickly. But as soon as we all admitted that we have feelings for each other and wanted to give this a go, I've felt it. I've never allowed myself to say it, but I know what love is. I know that I've never felt it until them. I know that I don't want to feel it for anyone but them. They are it for me.

"I didn't expect her to say those words," Matt says softly.

"Me either…"

Matt nods and runs his hand up and down my arm. "Did it feel right to you?"

"So right," I say honestly, and without any hesitation. I look up at him. "What about to you?"

"It felt right. I didn't think she'd be the first to say it, but fuck. It felt right." He leans down and kisses me. I can feel everything he feels in the kiss. The love courses through my veins and warms my soul.

I smile shyly when he pulls away. "We should probably put clothes on." I blush. "If we'll be having company."

He kisses my blush. "I'll order something." He stands and pulls me up with him. Keeping hold of my hand, he leads me upstairs as he orders from our favorite pizza place. Blaze has to make the best pizza in the world. I'd fight anyone who says otherwise.

Once we're cleaned up and dressed, I do what Mariah asked. I grab a pair of her sweats and a hoodie. I lay her favorite sweats and one of DJ's hoodies with his cologne sprayed on it on the bed and take the extras with me downstairs. When my chest feels like it's tightening again, I pull Matt's hoodie over my nose and inhale his spicy scent. Like DJ's does for both me and Mariah, Matt's scent is very calming.

I smile when Matt wraps his arms around me. "It's okay. Okay? Whatever is going on, we'll know soon."

"It has to be something bad. They would have called and told us they were going to be late. And shot at? Just... what?" I tighten my grip around his waist.

"Shh... Baby, it's okay." He tangles his fingers in my hair. "We know they're coming home. So we know they're okay."

I nod into his chest. "You're right."

"Mmhmm. I usually am."

I chuckle and look up at him. I stand on my tiptoes and kiss his jaw. I reach up and cup his cheek. He leans down and gives me the kiss I want just as there is a knock on the door. He taps my ass as he goes to answer it. I head for the kitchen to get things ready for us and our guest.

A few minutes later, I perk up at the sound of DJ's car pulling in the garage. I run to the door that connects the house to the garage and yank it open. DJ is helping an exhausted looking woman out of the car as Mariah is grabbing their gear from the trunk. I can see she's been crying. I hate that whatever happened, she dealt with it alone.

I quickly walk to her and take a bag. She gives me a soft, brave smile, but says nothing. I lean over and kiss her softly, rubbing my nose lovingly along hers just to tell her that she's okay now. That she's not alone anymore. Her eyes water as she takes a deep breath. I follow her and DJ along with the woman into the house.

DJ stops near the kitchen where Matt is standing by the counter arranging the boxes of pizza and other delicious food that has my stomach rumbling. Matt hands him the folded sweats and hoodie. DJ says nothing. He just takes them with a nod and leads the woman to one of the bathrooms.

A few moments later, he comes back and scrubs his hands down his face. "Where's Mariah?" he asks.

"Upstairs," I say quietly.

He leans down and kisses me softly. "I'll explain, baby. Just let us get settled."

I nod and nuzzle him, letting him know I understand. My heart really is racing. I hate everything about whatever is happening, even though I have no clue what exactly it is. I trust DJ, though. I know that he'll tell us what's going on as soon as he can. I'm sure he has reasons for waiting.

Once we're all gathered in the living room with our dinner, DJ clears his throat. "Matt. Lyric. This is Ms. Lamport."

"DeeDee. Please," she says softly. Her voice is kind. She's small, much like me and Mariah. "If this is where I am to stay for the time being, I'd like to be called DeeDee."

DJ nods. "Yes, ma'am." Mariah curls closer to him. I take that as a cue and snuggle closer to Matt.

"Thank you," she says just as softly as she begins to take small bites of her pizza.

"DeeDee is an inadvertent target in our war with Sergeant Isaac Jackson, and, as I found out tonight, Lieutenant Ben Prench." DJ kisses Mariah's head when she shivers.

My eyes widen, and I shake my head. "I... What happened? I don't understand." I cuddle into Matt as close as I can. Reading me well, he nudges me into his lap. I cuddle into him as he wraps a blanket around us.

DJ looks down at Mariah. "Do you want to begin with what happened?"

She shivers and grabs a blanket from the back of the couch as she shakes her head. "I really don't."

Following my lead, she crawls into DJ's lap and curls into him. DJ pulls the blanket tight around her as he hugs her as tightly as Matt is hugging me. We all continue to nibble on our dinner, though I'm sure it's out of necessity because none of us look hungry.

"Mariah got a call earlier to a disturbance. When she got there, she didn't see anything happening. The disturbance involved a guy on his porch screaming at people. He must have gone inside because when Mariah got there, he wasn't there. She went to the RP's house." DJ nods to DeeDee. "Ms. Lamport -"

"DeeDee," she whispers. "Please."

"Sorry." DJ smiles. "DeeDee let her in and told her that the guy had gone inside. He'd yelled at a few people. He screamed at a little girl walking her dog. A police officer showed up in an unmarked squad. DeeDee thought at first that he was there for the call. But then he parked his squad in the garage and went inside. It was alarming. Confusing. Mariah showed up not long afterwards and went to her house. She wasn't totally sure about her at first but decided to trust her."

"Good thing," DeeDee sniffles.

"She told Mariah that the person creating the disturbance had a lot of activity going on during the night. Cars coming and going. All hours."

"Drug house?" Matt asks.

"That's what Mariah thought. Probably correct," DJ confirms. "But things weren't adding up for her. The neighborhood was a good one. HOA type of neighborhood. Immaculate. Activity like that would be noticed. Probably was. But we had no reports of it. That's something else that threw her. She tried to call you, Matt. She didn't know that we'd sent you home. So she called me. Told me to look up her call. As soon as I saw the address, I swear I had a fucking heart attack. I told her to stay put. Don't do anything. I rushed out of the office to get to her as quickly as I could. I knew as soon as I saw the address that it was a set up."

My heart feels like it's in my throat, but I ask anyway. "Who was it?"

DJ closes his eyes a moment before looking back at us. He hugs Mariah tighter. "Isaac Jackson."

I gasp. "Oh, God."

Matt's fingertips dig into my sides as he growls. "Son... of... a bitch."

DJ nods. "That's not the worst part. I got there. Got the story. I told DeeDee not to approach him. I had intended to set up surveillance. Check in with DeeDee daily. I took Mariah out back with me to my squad. I didn't want her going out that front door to hers. Why they didn't try and take her when she arrived is something I don't know, but I wasn't taking any chances."

"We didn't know what a good idea that was at the time," Mariah says quietly.

I know I'm not going to like the rest of this. I shift and curl into Matt's chest. He wraps tighter around me and sways gently with me as he rubs up and down my arms, soothing me as much as he can.

DJ kisses Mariah's neck. "I stopped at the corner of the block to explain to her what was happening. Who the person creating the disturbance was. I told her about his past. The change."

"The accident," Matt says. DJ nods.

I look up at Matt. "Accident?"

Matt takes a breath and looks down at me. "Isaac was in an accident a few years ago. His kid and wife were killed. The person responsible was a female officer with our department. She was terminated. It was found that she had been negligent. She wasn't paying attention. Jackson was never the same afterwards."

"I… didn't know that…," I whisper. My heart aches for the guy. Losing his whole family had to be so hard. I don't know what I would do if I ever lost DJ, Matt, or Mariah. It's devastating and heartbreaking to think about.

DJ takes another breath. "It changed him. But he managed to make it seem like he was coping. Yes, he'd become a pretty big dick, but for the most part, he did his job. We didn't have a huge amount of complaints against him." He rubs his temple. "DeeDee called dispatch and was transferred to my squad just about the time I finished telling Mariah what happened, and who her RP was calling about. DeeDee was calling to warn us that Jackson had a gun aimed at us. She just got the words out when shots were fired at us. I moved just in time."

Mariah and I both burst into tears at the same time. Matt pulls me into his chest and tangles his fingers into my hair. I grip the waistband of his sweats as I sob into his chest. I knew. I knew it. I absolutely knew something bad had happened. I felt it. I've felt like God's hand itself had started squeezing my heart and hadn't let go all afternoon.

"Fucking hell," Matt says into my hair. He nudges me up and guides me to the other couch. I sit next to DJ and Mariah. I hug them both as Mariah and I both cry. Matt wraps around us both. I look up when I hear DeeDee sniffle.

Before I can say anything though, DJ holds out an arm. DeeDee doesn't waste time, and it goes to show just how scary the entire situation must be for her. She cuddles into us like she's known us all of our lives.

"Isaac started running across the street to DeeDee's house," DJ continues. "We didn't know who the other cop was then, but he followed. DeeDee was able to identify him. She'd seen him running at her clear as day. Mariah and I sped away and got her from the back of her house. Isaac aimed at DeeDee while she was running. I didn't have a shot. Mariah did, though. She shot him in the shoulder, we think. Prench pulled Jackson away. We didn't see him at that time. Just saw whoever it was had a uniform on."

"DJ, why didn't one of you call?" Matt asks.

"Because we couldn't. I sent in SWAT and got us out of there as fast as I could. We left Mariah's squad. Which was shot up worse than my vehicle. Her cell was in there. We didn't get it back until Blake brought it to us. I got pulled in many different directions. Mariah got pulled into several different interviews. When she finally called you, she was in a meeting with me and the Chief. She actually got up and said she was done with interviews. She wanted to go home. She's said everything that happened many times in front of a camera. She did her statement. She said she was done and needed to call her loves. Chief King's mouth fell open in shock, but that was the end of it."

"How did you find out about Prench?" Matt asks as he keeps us all as close as he can.

"We knew there was an unmarked car out there with a crooked cop. DeeDee told me she'd gotten a good look at him. After she had finally calmed down enough to think about what happened, she was pretty convinced she could identify him. So I showed her the department photos of the four cops we had in unmarked cars that day. She identified Prench. When he didn't come back to the department at what would have been the end of his shift, her identification was even more confirmed. He's also one of Jackson's best friends. They went through the academy together. They were partners for a long time. We got a warrant and sent out SWAT to Prench's house. He's not there." DJ sighs.

"There's more…," I whisper. I don't need to ask.

DJ kisses the top of my head as I hug him and Mariah both tighter. "We don't know where either of them are. We're searching, but so far we've come up empty. We have some of our investigators on the case. The whole department is working on this. But that means that you and Mariah are targets. It means DeeDee was thrown into this inadvertently. We need to operate like she's also a target. She has no family in the area. She doesn't have friends that she can turn to in this situation. She trusts us. With Lyric still on injury leave and Mariah being suspended for discharging her weapon, that leaves the three of you here alone. I don't like it."

"I'll go on leave," Matt says. I don't want him to be out of work. He loves his job, but hearing that he'll go on leave makes me feel better. It's not that I don't think Mariah and I can handle it. I know we can. But I don't feel like being brave right now.

"I'm glad you said that," DJ says. "The choices were you going on leave or us suspending you for longer for the Jackson incident. The problem with that idea is that we would have to put it in your jacket as a disciplinary action, and none of us thought that was right. The Chief couldn't get around that."

"I'll take the leave. I'm not leaving these three here alone without backup, and you're needed at the department. You have more pull in certain areas than I do, so you should be there."

DJ nods. "With that settled, I'd like to get DeeDee settled in the guest room. We'll get everything down here cleaned up. Dishes. Pizza boxes. All of that."

We all take a few deep breaths before any of us move, but we eventually do what he asks us to. Matt and I stay downstairs with Mariah and clean up from our dinner. DJ takes DeeDee upstairs and gets her comfortable.

Once we're all done with our tasks, we make our way to DJ's bedroom. We've all come to think of his home and bedroom as ours. We've all moved most of our things over here over the past several weeks. Matt and DJ have been talking about what to do with Matt's house. DJ's is larger. It's where we've all grown comfortable and spent the most time.

Once we've all gone through our routine for bed, though, we realize we need the reassurance that Mariah and DJ are really okay. Sleep would never come easy to us without it. So we all climb into bed and spend hours making love. We take the comfort we need from one another before we finally fall into an exhausted tangle of limbs and fall asleep wrapped in each other.

Chapter Fifteen

☆ Matt ☆

(Two Days Later)

I yawn as I stretch out on the pool chair and watch Lyric swim leisure laps in the pool. It's been a couple of days since Mariah and DJ had been shot at. I'm far more angry than I was after I'd heard about it. If I come face to face with Jackson or Prench, neither of them will have to worry about facing the legal system. They'll both come against my own personal form of justice.

Lyric flips and starts floating on her back. I smile when she closes her eyes. I can see her relax. Tension she's felt over the past couple of days melts from her body. She starts to smile softly as she floats.

The girl is truly beautiful. Her sun-kissed skin glows and shimmers as the sun hits the water. Her purple bikini hugs her body. She loves the color. It's her favorite. I love the color because it looks amazing on her. I'm sure it's because she feels gorgeous in it. The truth is, she's just a gorgeous woman. I'm a lucky man to be one of the people she chose as her life partners.

Just as I'm about to jump in the pool and show her what she means to me, Mariah straddles me and kisses me long and very deeply. Her tongue tangles with mine. My hands automatically move to her ass as she lets out a small whimper in response to my moan.

My reaction to these girls and DJ is nothing short of astounding. I've never reacted to anyone the way I do to them. I just need to be in the same room with them, and my entire body buzzes with the need to touch them. Be close. It's hard to hide the blood that rushes directly to my dick and makes me solid as titanium for them.

Mariah knows far too well what she does to me. Lyric has learned quickly. DJ loves to take full advantage of it. Mariah is far more shy about telling me what she wants. It's very rare for her to just take what she needs. But I've learned her signs. She's pressing herself down against my dick right now. I'm not the type of person who would ever not give my girl what she needs, but I do pull slightly away and still her hips when she starts grinding against me.

"Baby," I say deeply against her lips. I smile at her whimper. "We have a guest, sweet girl. Fucking you right now when she can come outside and see might not be the greatest idea."

"Then take me somewhere she won't see…" Her eyes glimmer with heat.

"Breakfast is ready!" DeeDee yells from the door. Mariah deflates.

I chuckle. "I love you, baby. But later. I promise."

"I don't know what's wrong with me. I had DJ before he left for work. Lyric and I fucked around before she got up. I'm insatiable today."

I laugh. "I don't get an insatiable Mariah very often." I slap her ass. She giggles. "Let's grab breakfast. I'll help out with the sexual appetite after. Though, between you and Lyric today, you're going to exhaust me. She had me twice in that pool."

Mariah laughs as she gets up. "Poor Matt." She reaches out a hand for me.

I laugh and take her hand, letting her help me up. I kiss the top of her head before grabbing a towel for Lyric. I wrap it around her as soon as she's out of the pool and pull her into a hug that has her giving me a content sigh.

I kiss the top of her head. "Feel better?"

"So much better. That was a really good idea."

"I tend to have them from time to time," I drawl, knowing she can't resist my Southern accent.

She giggles and playfully swats my arm as she kisses my chest. "I really love you."

"I really love you, too. Let's get breakfast. Now that we have your back feeling better, we should get you fed."

"Really. Thank you for suggesting it. I don't know why it hurt so bad this morning."

I pull away and take her hand. "Because you've been beyond tense, honey. We all have. You're bound to feel some muscle tension." I lead her into the house where Mariah is happily sitting at the table with a waffle.

She looks up at us with wide eyes. "Oh my God. She made waffles and bacon!"

I laugh. "Rih's favorite." I smile and look at DeeDee. "We might never allow you to leave if you keep cooking our favorite foods."

DeeDee laughs and sits down next to Mariah. "It's the least I can do to repay the kindness. It means so much to me that you are allowing me to stay here. I don't think I've ever felt so safe."

Lyric smiles as she heads for the bathroom to dry off. I dish up and sit on the other side of Mariah. "We're happy to do it," I say as I start eating.

"You all have done so much over the past couple of days. Having the officers get some of my belongings was honestly so wonderful of you."

"We're happy to, DeeDee. I don't know if DJ and I would still be here without you," Mariah says quietly.

I reach down and grip her bare thigh. I love when she wears the short jean cut-offs that she's wearing right now. I lean over and kiss her cheek as I lightly rub my thumb over her smooth skin. A few minutes later, Lyric sits on the other side of me shyly. I kiss her forehead and smile when she blushes.

Later, after all is cleaned up and put away, DeeDee finds a quiet place in the shade and starts reading a Stephen King book that she's borrowed from Mariah. Lyric and Mariah have decided on a pool day, so they've both put their bikinis on.

I didn't realize it, but they match. Mariah's is pink, but it's the exact same string bikini that leaves nothing to the imagination. It barely covers her. I decide then and there that they aren't allowed to wear them for anyone but me and DJ. They look far too good. I know if I caught anyone else looking at them, the possessive asshole I am would definitely come out to play. They're mine and DJ's. For our eyes only.

I laugh when Lyric runs by Mariah in a blur and jumps in the pool. Mariah's eyes widen in shock. "Cold, baby?" I ask when Lyric resurfaces.

She nods with adorably large cub-like eyes. "So cold. I didn't expect my suit would be that cold. It's eighty degrees out here!"

I laugh again. "Eighty out here. Sixty-eight in there."

She shakes her head and hugs herself. "That needs to change. Immediately. Mariah and I get control of the temperature."

I sit down on the edge of the pool. "Not a chance in hell. That's fucking sacred."

Mariah sits next to me. "Besides. I think anything more than sixty-eight would just be uncomfortable."

Lyric looks at her with a playful pout. "You're meant to be on my side."

Mariah giggles. "Not when it comes to controlling the temperature in the house. You'd have it at eighty in there."

Lyric playfully turns up her nose. "Because I'm the only one with any sense."

Mariah and I both laugh. Lyric splashes us both and dives under the water before we have a chance to retaliate. I look at Mariah. She gives me a sad look as if she's been betrayed, but I can see the smile underneath.

"We can't allow this," I tell her.

She shakes her head. "Nope. We can't. She must pay for such a blatant act of treachery." She frowns sadly. "It's the only option." She looks at Lyric as she resurfaces on the other side of the pool. She casually leans against it and blinks at us.

"How should we play this?" I whisper conspiringly.

She giggles. "I follow you, fearless leader."

I laugh. "Okay. We flank her. She'll try to dart ahead of us to avoid it, but we'll be expecting that. We'll both cut her off and catch her. We'll haul her back to the farthest corner of the pool. We'll cover our illicit intentions by hiding her as we finger fuck an apology out of her."

She laughs. "Sir, yes sir!"

I grin a little evilly at our plan. "Ready? Break!"

We both slide into the pool. We slowly stalk her like she's our prey. She watches us carefully with a slightly tilted head. When we get about halfway across the pool, she pulls herself out. I narrow my eyes. I didn't count on her doing that. Lyric stands and looks at us.

"Now what, Lieutenant?" Mariah whispers.

I think quickly before leaning over and whispering in her ear. "We split up. You stay in the pool. I'll get out."

She smiles. "Okay. Good idea. You're the fastest runner." She casually starts swimming.

I swim to the edge of the pool closest to the house and pull myself out just as she tries darting past me. I knew she'd attempt to get to the house, which is the reason I chose that side of the pool to get out of.

But I'm faster. I have far longer legs. Just as she reaches the door, I catch her arm.

"No!" she shrieks.

I grin as she tries to pull away, but I'm too close now. I grab her around the waist, and in one swift motion, I throw her over my shoulder. "You're in trouble now." I swat her ass.

"Matt! Don't you dare! What are you doing?" She grips the waistband of my shorts as she wiggles and squirms, trying to get me to let her down.

I laugh. "So much trouble, little girl."

"Matt!" she laughs as I tickle her. She wiggles more, but lets go of my shorts just as I jump into the pool. She screams when I shift her as we hit the water. She gets away from me, but I always have a plan. She ends up in Mariah's arms.

"Hey, my love." Mariah giggles as she kisses her neck and locks her in her arms.

Lyric squeaks in surprise as she tries to get free. Mariah has a vice-like grip, though. "Traitor!" Lyric squawks as Mariah starts to propel them both to the farthest corner of the pool.

"Score one for Team Matt," I say huskily against her ear as I press her against the wall of the pool.

She shivers. "Not fair. I was tag teamed."

"Oh, you're about to be," Mariah whispers against Lyric's lips before she kisses her.

"Fucking hell, that's hot," I say as I glance over my shoulder. If DeeDee has any idea what's happening, she's ignoring it. I turn back to Lyric and slide my hand into her bikini bottoms as Mariah kisses her senseless.

"Oh…," Lyric moans. She braces herself against the pool's edge as Mariah pulls away.

Mariah slides her hand into Lyric's bikini bottoms. We both watch Lyric as we each slide one finger into her pussy. We thrust hard and deep in simultaneous motions. Lyric moans quietly and lets her head fall back as she enjoys the pleasure we're giving her.

Lyric arches into our fingers. I set my thumb against her clit just as Mariah and I start to crook our fingers against her G-spot. It causes her to let out an adorable sigh before she bites her lip and closes her eyes. Her pussy clenches around our fingers and pulses for us.

I glance over my shoulder again. DeeDee is paying no attention to us. I grin and thrust harder, deeper, and faster. Mariah follows my lead. We know exactly what our girl likes. As we thrust and continue to crook our fingers against her spot, we lean forward and kiss her neck. She moans quietly in pleasure. I rub her clit in faster circles. I give her a little more pressure as Mariah starts rubbing her thumb from Lyric's clit to her pussy while we thrust.

"Shit…," Lyric whispers.

Mariah and I both nip her neck. Lyric's pussy tightens and begins a delectable, erratic pulsing around our fingers. She lets out quiet whimpers and sighs of ecstasy. I can see her arms start to tremble.

I kiss up her neck to her ear. "Tell us what you want, baby," I whisper.

"I want to come for you," she whispers. She leans towards me when Mariah kisses up her neck to her ear. We both continue giving her hard, deep, and fast thrusts while we crook our fingers.

"Not until you apologize for your act of treason." Mariah shakes her head with an evil grin. " Splashing us."

Lyric's eyes widen. "What?" She rides our fingers clenching just as tight around them as she does around my dick.

I smile. "You heard her. You want to come? You better say sorry."

"Oh…," Lyric moans quietly and shakes her head.

I look at Mariah. "She's going to make it hard."

Mariah grins and starts thrusting harder and faster. "Then I guess we have to make it harder."

I lean in and kiss her deeply. Mariah kisses her neck. Lyric whimpers and writhes and moans. We continue to thrust hard, deep, and fast, but we also start twisting our fingers in opposite directions as we crook them against her spot. I rub her clit faster with the amount of pressure I know she likes. Mariah keeps rubbing from her clit to her pussy at the same pace I'm rubbing.

Lyric trembles and clamps hard around us. She's not going to last. Her eyes widen just as I feel her start to pulse erratically. She knows if she comes, she'll face a punishment. Her decision is will the punishment be worth it, or should she just apologize and enjoy the ride she's about to take?

After tormenting herself a few moments, Lyric can't take anymore. "Okay… I'm sorry. Please let me come." She looks up at us through her lashes as submissively as she can. Her pussy is spasming around us as the control she's managing to hold onto nearly slips from her grasp.

Mariah flicks her pussy as I flick her clit. Lyric jerks into us. "Come for us, sexy girl," Mariah whispers.

Lyric grips the pools edge and lets her head fall back again. She lets out another quiet moan. "Oh, fuck." Her pussy clamps down on our fingers. She comes hard. I can feel wave after wave of her release as Mariah and I slow our thrusts and rubs.

"Such a good little girl for us." I glance back over my shoulder. DeeDee is still not paying us any mind.

"A very, very good girl." Mariah kisses Lyric again, softly this time as we both stop thrusting while Lyric comes down.

After a few moments, we both pull out of her slowly. She looks at us both blushing a beautiful shade of red. We both lean in and kiss her blush then take off in the pool laughing as she watches us, dazed.

I love days like this. Days where we can all just be with each other. Like we have no cares in the world. Despite the shit that looms over us, the fact that we can destress is something that we absolutely need.

Later that day, after DJ gets home, we decide on a barbecue. I make steaks and grilled vegetables. Lyric and Mariah make a fruit salad. We continue our carefree day until the sun sets. As we all crawl into bed, I'm thankful to see they're all exhausted.

With my girls and DJ wrapped in my arms, we all fall into the first restful sleep we've had in days. Maybe even weeks.

I couldn't be more grateful.

Chapter Sixteen

☆ Mariah ☆

(One Month Later)

I sigh and flip over onto my stomach. I turn the page of the newest Nora Roberts book and pout. Usually, I can lose myself in her writing. It's one of the greatest things about incredible writers. The ability for readers to lose themselves.

Unfortunately, Ms. Roberts isn't helping me today. Not in the slightest. I've read an entire chapter, but as I reach the end, I honestly have no idea what I just read. I close the book, giving up. There's no point.

I put my head in my hands and let the sun beat down on my back. It's been nearly a month since Isaac Jackson and Ben Prench shot at us. They've been underground. DJ hasn't heard anything from them. It's unsettling. None of us like how they've just disappeared.

DJ also can't justify us being off any longer. Lyric is healed. She's been cleared to go back to work. I was cleared long ago after the mandatory investigation that automatically happens after cops discharge their weapon. I have no more personal time I can take. The department is starting to come down on Matt for being on leave so long. They want us all back, and we're running out of excuses not to be.

Even DeeDee couldn't justify being here anymore. While we all had grown to think of her as family, and she sort of thought of us all as her kids, even we had to admit there was no reason she couldn't go home. Her home had been fixed up and cleaned out.

The surveillance we had set up around her house to keep a look out for Isaac couldn't even be truly justified any longer. The house remained quiet. No one had come in or out of it. Even the surveillance around Ben's house yielded absolutely nothing. They're just gone.

I sigh as I adjust the chair slightly so my head is elevated a little to compensate for the triple D balls hanging from my chest. Laying flat on my stomach makes me feel like I'm choking on my own tits.

I squeak out a scream when I feel a hand come down on my pink bikini clad ass. I turn towards the source of the swat, catching my breath. DJ grins at me as he adjusts the chair next to me. He sits down and pops a pair of Aviator sunglasses on.

"Are you trying to give me a heart attack?" I reach over and swat his leg with a smile.

He shrugs and gives me a sexy smile. "Couldn't help it. You look sexy as fuck laying in my yard on my pool chair."

I laugh. "Yours. Yours. Yours." I shake my head in mock exasperation. "So cocky."

"Fuck right."

I giggle. "So all of the stuff we've all brought in over the past couple of months since we've moved in. Yours?"

"Well, you all are mine, honey. So, yeah. I'd say it's all mine."

I crack up. "I'd love to see you in this pink bikini. Though, I don't think you'll fit. Your dick is too big. It would just hang out with your balls. And your chest is definitely not big enough to fill the cups."

He laughs. "You don't think my pectoral muscles would fill the cups?"

"Not a chance in hell, DJ. I definitely have bigger balls than you." I turn and adjust my chair so I can sit up next to him.

He laughs as he unabashedly stares at my chest. I blush under the heat of his gaze. "I can't deny that." His husky drawl sends shivers directly between my thighs. But I shouldn't be surprised at that. DJ, Matt, and Lyric all do things to me that no one has ever done before.

I've never opened myself up to anyone the way I have them. The one person I tried to with was too selfish to really listen to me. In any manner. The bedroom and otherwise. I was stupid to believe he would. There were so many signs before I really got too deeply involved with him. But I didn't listen to them. Instead, I jumped in head first and believed all of his lies. When I finally came out on the other side, I was a different person.

Truthfully, I still struggle with the damage he caused. I'm not the same confident person I used to be. I struggle hard with believing I'm a good person. I struggle even harder with believing I'm beautiful in any manner.

Which is why when DJ, Matt, or Lyric look at me like they want to devour me, my heart races out of control, and I feel like I'm going to throw up. I don't have to look at DJ to know he's looking me up and down. The fire in his eyes is leaving scorch marks on my skin. It's like I'm being sucked into the sun and burning up the closer I get. It's both exciting and scary as hell.

DJ reaches over and takes my hand. I bite my lip as the blush spreads across my cheeks. He tugs me gently. I obey the silent command and get up. I refuse to meet his eyes, though, because I know I'll burst into an unnamed shade of deep red.

"Come here, baby. Tell me what's going on behind those beautiful eyes of yours." He adjusts his chair so he's laying down with his head slightly elevated and gently guides me down so I'm straddling him.

I cuddle into him with my head tucked under his chin. "I'm scared. Honestly. Jackson and Prench just disappeared. It's scary. It makes no sense. How do they just vanish?"

DJ wraps his arms around me. "I wish like hell I had answers for you, baby. I wish I could tell you that I think it's over. Realistically, I don't. I think they're waiting to make their move. I think we need to be prepared, and on guard. I don't like the fact that we can't just keep the two of you here with me or Matt until we catch them."

I sigh. "Honestly, I think both of us are ready to get back. I think we're both getting a little sick of sitting at home."

DJ chuckles. "If you think I can't see that, you're crazy, baby girl."

I smile and look up at him. I kiss his jaw. "One thing I am glad about, though. I've become comfortable with who I am over the past couple of months. Loving Lyric as much as I love you and Matt. I know it's not wrong."

"There is never anything wrong with love. You can't control your heart, baby."

"I think seeing you and Matt with each other has helped a lot. The two of you expressing your love so freely. And Lyric being able to freely show me what I mean to her. I feel really lucky that the people I love have helped not only show me who I am, but also to not be afraid to show others who I am."

DJ smiles and tangles his fingers in my hair with one hand. The other trails a delicious path down my back to my ass and back. He kisses me so lovingly and sweetly, I melt into him, unquestioning of his love. He grips my ass and deepens the kiss, trailing his tongue over mine. He sucks lightly on my lower lip when he pulls away slowly.

As usual, my body feels like it ignites for him. It always does for him, Matt, and Lyric. The feeling is so sweet and sexy that it always sends chills throughout my being. I feel like my body warms with tingles.

He groans as he pulls away slightly. I feel him harden underneath me. I love the effect I have on him. It's one of the things that makes me feel sexy when I'm having trouble believing it. The way he looks at me makes me feel pretty in ways I never thought possible.

"This is going to go a lot farther if I don't pull away now," he whispers against my lips.

I smile because he knows me very well. I'm not the type of person who is capable of sexual activity every day. It's another thing I've always found to be an embarrassment about myself. Clit sensitivity. What the hell even is that?

"I'm okay," I whisper back. Despite the fact we all spent last night with each other, I'm not as sensitive as I thought I'd be today.

He narrows his eyes. "Are you sure? Because I know you. You'd probably let me fuck you just because you know it would make me happy and relieve the hard on you're feeling underneath you."

I giggle and push myself down against him. I slowly grind over on his dick with what I hope is a seductive and sultry look. Just the feel of him between my thighs makes my desire for him reach heights that I'm still not used to.

DJ groans and shifts. He tugs his shorts down and pushes my bikini bottoms aside. Seconds later, he's filling me in ways only he knows how. He pushes my hair behind my ear as I adjust to his size. He and Matt are both so large that it always takes me a minute to stretch around them.

Like he always does, DJ watches me for my sign that I'm ready for him to move. I don't know what it is, but he does. He never starts thrusting until I'm ready. I never have to say a word to him or move myself. DJ just knows.

He leans in and kisses me as he starts thrusting slowly and deep. I let out a content moan and close my eyes. I wrap my arms around his shoulders and let him take me to the clouds. He wraps his arms around me and holds me tightly as the love he has for me seeps into my bones. I feel him so deeply, I know his imprint will be on me forever.

He breathes against my neck as he kisses it. He moves slowly, but every thrust of his thick cock inside me brings me closer and closer to the freefall with him that I desire. My body trembles as my pussy clenches and pulses around him. I get tighter and tighter. DJ never thrusts faster, though, I'm sure he wants to. I can feel the restraint, and I'm grateful for it.

He knows he could pound himself into me right now and satisfy me just as much, but it's not what I need. I need him. I need to feel him. I need to feel his heart. What could be a hot quickie in the backyard under the heat of the Florida sun is anything but. It's a full-fledged lovemaking session that I feel in the very core of me.

When I get to the point of no return, I feel tears sting my eyes. They shock me because they aren't tears of sadness. They're tears of love. Like I feel it so deeply that it's overflowing from me. I hold him tighter when I feel him tighten his grip.

"Come for me, my beautiful girl," he whispers.

I bury my face in his neck just as he holds himself as deeply in me as he can. We both fall at the same time. Our hips jerk hard against each other. He fills me with hot jets of himself. I take it all. My pussy intensely pulses around him, squeezing him until he's given me everything.

"DJ...," I whisper as I melt completely into him.

He smiles against my neck and tugs my hair so I'm looking at him. He licks and kisses my tears until I'm smiling and giggling. He sits up with me, still buried deep inside my pussy. I stay wrapped around him.

"You okay?" he asks me. He kisses me softly.

I smile. "I am. That's exactly what I needed. I don't know how you, Matt, or Lyric do that. You all read me so well and always manage to give me what I need. Even if I don't really know what that is."

He smiles. "Well, that's our job, baby. You do the same for us. Even if you don't know it."

We both stay in each other's arms, but turn towards the door of the house as a squealing Lyric runs out of it. Matt follows, close on her heels. Lyric looks over her shoulder and runs around the far side of the pool.

Matt chases her. "You can't possibly think you're getting away with that, little one!"

Lyric screams as Matt reaches her just as she nears us. "Matt! No!"

He grabs her around the waist and hauls her against his chest. He lifts her off the ground as she squeals and wiggles to get away. "Oh, yes."

"What was the offense, Lieutenant?" DJ asks with a grin.

"Little brat ate the last of the jerky and didn't replace it or bother to put it on the shopping list. It's fucking on," Matt answers as he walks her to the pool. She does all she can to get away, but she's no match for Matt's strength.

"I'm sorry!" She squawks and giggles while she pushes at his arms.

"Too late. The offense happened. Time to face the consequences," Matt says.

"A jerky offense," I say, giggling. "The punishment must be swift."

"Swift and just!" DJ puts in. "The only option is the pool. She must be thrown in."

Lyric's eyes widen when Matt prepares to toss her into the water. "Matt! No! I'm still fully clothed!"

"Should've thought of that before you decided to pop that last piece of delectable meat into your sexy little mouth." Matt launches a flailing Lyric into the pool.

DJ winks at me and pulls out slowly. I moan at the loss, but watch him curiously as he shifts me off him. He stealthily sneaks up behind Matt, who is watching Lyric resurface. Lyric pushes her hair from her eyes. When she sees what DJ is about to do, she gets an evil grin on her face. I put my hand over my mouth to keep from laughing because I know Matt is probably giving her a baffled look right now.

Matt takes a cautious step back and starts to glance over his shoulder. Just when his eyes meet DJ's, DJ pushes him in the pool. Lyric and I both crack up as Matt flails, much like Lyric did, as he hits the water.

When he resurfaces, he sputters out water. "The fuck was that about?"

"I can't just do nothing in the way of redeeming my girl's honor," DJ says calmly.

It's then I make my own move. Matt grins when he sees me running silently towards DJ. Lyric's mouth drops, but before she has a chance to warn him, I send DJ flying into the pool with a victorious giggle.

Matt cracks up as DJ resurfaces and gives me a betrayed look. "That's my girl!" Matt cheers.

I do a victory dance that doesn't last long. DJ quickly swims to the side of the pool and pulls himself out. I squeak and take off running for the house, but outrunning him was never going to happen. He's just as fast as Matt is.

He catches me quickly and throws me over his shoulder. "Battle lines have been drawn," he growls sexily.

"Matt!" I squawk for help.

"I'm coming, baby gi-" Matt is cut off just as I feel DJ sailing through the air.

I hit the water with him and see Matt in a splashing battle with Lyric. DJ lets me go and takes position next to Lyric. He gangs up with her against Matt. I quickly swim to Matt's side and start helping him.

"Let the battle begin!" I yell.

Matt and I launch an all-out splashing war against Lyric and DJ. We all laugh and chase each other until we're all exhausted.

When we finally manage to climb out of the pool, DJ puts up a frame tent for us to sit under out of the sun. Matt starts barbecuing after he and Lyric change. We all stay out relaxing with each other until the sun is long set.

Tomorrow, when we all have to go back to work and face reality, seems so distant that we all almost forget there is still a dangerous force looming over us.

A dark presence watching us from whatever corner of Hell he's hiding in.

Chapter Seventeen

☆ *DJ* ☆

"Well, my girls are out there today. So, we need to figure this shit out," I say to Blake.

"DJ, fuck. I know, okay? I'm just relaying to you the information I got from my CI."

I sigh. Blake is also on my taskforce. I just added him not long ago. I needed someone who has the ability to talk to anyone and get information. Blake is, for reasons I don't understand, liked by everyone. Women think he's hot. Men want to be him or something. I don't know. What I do know is he is able to get information I need that I'd never be able to get without him.

Like today.

His confidential informant is probably some college kid or something. So far, this person has managed to get us a lot of shit. There is an influx of a drug called XANG. From what I know, it's some kind of mix of Ecstasy and PCP. It's also known as Angel's X.

It seems perfect for college kids, but a fucking nightmare for us. Now, we have a bunch of college partiers running around hallucinating about magical dragons and humping telephone poles. But they're strong as hell and difficult as a fucking dragon to control.

Ecstasy typically raises a person's body temperature and increases their want and need to be sexual. PCP is a dissociative drug that typically makes people feel like they aren't in their own body. Taken in high doses, though, it can make them hallucinate. It also gives them serious levels of adrenaline. So while they have no idea what's happening around them, they end up having almost superhuman strength.

These two drugs mixed together has been causing users to hallucinate while being very sexual. One of the biggest issues is that if the other person isn't a consenting party, they aren't able to get away. We've had reports of both men and women sexual assault victims. Many of the assailants we've found have been coming down from the drug having no memory of their actions. Some we've caught up to while they are still under the effects of the drugs.

I have a report in front of me from Blake regarding one such situation. The woman reported her ex-boyfriend came onto her at a party they had both attended. After the assault, she immediately went to her current boyfriend for help. Her boyfriend called the police. He led them straight to her ex. When my officers tried to apprehend him, they couldn't control him. The taser didn't work. Mase didn't work. Striking him with batons, or even fists, didn't work.

One of the officers finally ended up shooting him because he'd managed to gain control of another officer's weapon and began firing it. He was shot seven times before he finally went down. Four of our officers were injured. One was shot in the leg. Everyone ended up okay except for the assailant. He didn't make it.

I run my hands down my face. "I wasn't prepared for this today."

"How do you want to play this, Cap?"

I look at him for a moment before shaking my head. "We don't have a fucking choice. We have to act. We don't have time to set up the surveillance I want to." I reach for my office phone and dial Matt's extension.

"Chance," he growls.

"My office," I say before hanging up. I stand and pace. "I wanted to find him. I'm glad you did, but this isn't how I wanted this to go down."

"I know," Blake says. "I fucking know it. But you're right. We need to act."

I glance at my door as Matt slips in. He closes it behind him and gives me a quick kiss. I don't know if he knew it would go a long way in calming me down, or if he just did it. But as he sits, my heart rate slows slightly.

"What's going on?" Matt asks.

"We found Jackson and Prench," I say. I hand him Blake's report.

Matt looks at it apprehensively when neither of us say anything more. When he's done reading it, he leans back. "Fuck me." He rubs his eyes. "Walk me through that. Just so I make sure I understand what I just fucking read."

Blake chuckles. "Oh, you understood it. But okay. I'll walk you through it. Last night, I went out on patrol. I decided to check in with my CI. There was a party going on at one of the frat houses. He's a member. Just as I was about to call him, he called me. Said his friend's girlfriend had been sexually assaulted. The person who did it was her ex. He was hopped up on the new drug we've been chasing down. XANG. I showed up after other officers. We had a fuck of a time wrangling him."

Matt waves a hand. "Yeah. Got that part."

Blake leans forward and rests his elbows on his knees. "I pulled my CI aside. Asked if he had any idea where the drugs came from. He said he was going to call me anyway. He'd tracked down the source."

"Your CI has told us twelve times he's tracked the source," Matt says, glaring.

"Yeah. But this time, he really fucking did. We were able to arrest two more guys last night who wouldn't give up the dealer, but my CI led me right to the dealer's house." Blake looks over at Matt. "Ben fucking Prench and Isaac fucking Jackson."

Matt looks at me. "How is this possible? We had surveillance on both of their houses for a month."

I shrug. "My guess is they knew. Or they have contacts within the department still."

"Fuck. Don't. Don't fucking say that." Matt stands and runs his fingers through his hair. "Fucking hell."

"If I hadn't seen them with my own eyes, I wouldn't believe it," Blake says. "But I did. I watched a deal go down."

"I'm getting a warrant," I say. "I texted the girls. They should be here soon. Hopefully, we'll have the warrant by then. Blake texted a few of our SWAT guys. The ones who aren't working today. We're going to meet at our house. Mobilize from there."

Matt shakes his head. "Fuck, I need to think."

I stand. "Think on the way. We all need the time to wrap our minds around this shit. We'll take my squad since it's new and more comfortable than either of yours." I try to give them a teasing smile, but it doesn't reach my eyes.

We all walk out to my squad in silence. The silence stretches all the way home. We're all lost in thought. I find myself wondering how I'm not more excited that Jackson and Prench just fell into our laps.

The truth is, I'm terrified. The fact that they end up being seen at Prench's house not long after we pulled surveillance is disturbing. We've only been off them for a week. Either they've been watching us, or we have a bigger fucking problem. A problem I don't want to think about.

When I pull up to our house, Lyric and Mariah are already there. The three of us pile out of my squad. Matt and I both beeline for our girls and wrap them in our arms. I don't care who is watching. I know Blake doesn't give a shit, but I have nosy neighbors just like everyone else. People like drama. They like gossip. But as I breathe in Mariah's and Lyric's sweet scent, all of that fades far into the back of my mind.

"What's happening?" Lyric asks quietly.

I take a breath. "We found Jackson and Prench. And they're wrapped up in some really fucked up shit."

Matt and I both pull slightly away as our girls look up at us with adorable confused looks. Matt runs his fingers through his hair. "That new drug popping up all over the fucking place is being supplied by them."

Mariah just blinks. "How... do you know they're supplying it?"

"Because my CI got information and led me right to them," Blake says. He's leaning against the bumper bars on the front of my squad.

Mariah shakes her head like she's coming out of a daze. "That's not how drug rings work."

"We've taken out several dealers over the past month, Rih," Blake says. "I assure you. They're the end of the line."

"No, wait," Lyric says, glancing at Mariah. "They might be the big suppliers, but who supplies them?"

Blake chuckles. "They're manufacturing it in Prench's garage. We didn't get a chance to do a lot of surveillance, and I wouldn't believe it if I didn't see it, but I swear to fucking God."

"He's right, baby. He got a pic of it. It's in his report. He took it with his cellphone." I hold out my hand. Blake gives me the phone with the image already pulled up. I show it to Matt, Lyric, and Mariah. "I couldn't believe what I was seeing either, but it's there. In living color."

"Jesus God in Heaven," Mariah mumbles.

I glance up and hand Blake his phone back as someone pulls in my driveway. I'm relieved to see my team arriving so quickly. I want this over with as soon as possible, but I want to be able to do at least a little surveillance. I don't want to go in if it's more than the two of them there. Not that we couldn't handle it.

The problem is Lyric and Mariah. I'm overly protective of them. What they've been through isn't something anyone should go through. But they're more than just partners on my team. They're partners in life. I love them.

It's more than just them. It's also Matt. I love all of them. I don't want them in harm's way. I don't want to walk in there worrying about losing the loves of my life. I intend on marrying them. All of them. Legally, I know I can only marry one, but I'll have a ceremony that signifies a union between us all. I don't care that we've only been together a few months. I know where I'm at. I know what I want. I know they all feel the same as I do.

"I got the warrant," Joe says, handing it to me.

I look it over. "Garage and house. We're looking for the drugs, drug paraphernalia, supplies used to make the drugs, money, storing equipment, and equipment used to manufacture. We're looking for lists of the dealers. Anyone else they supply to. We're taking weapons. Specifically the automatic that he used to fire on us. We're taking computers and phones." I look up at Joe. "You got my arrest warrants?"

"No, sir. Paul is coming with them."

I nod. "Everyone gear up. When the team gets here, I'll brief everyone at the same time." I head for my squad.

Matt follows. "What are we planning?"

"We need to spend some time surveilling. It's Friday. There has to be parties going on. I'm sure they'll be handing out their product left and right."

"DJ?" Lyric asks quietly when she appears at my side.

I look down at her. "Yeah, baby?"

"What about DeeDee? She's still a target."

"I was actually thinking about her," Matt says. "What about Quinn? He comes in from her direction. We could have him grab her on his way here. She can stay in the house."

"I'd feel better about it," Lyric says. "I just don't like the idea that they've resurfaced, and she's alone."

I nod. "Call her. Tell her we have Quinn coming for her. Matt. Call Quinn. I see Paul coming up the street. I want to look at the arrest warrant."

Matt and Lyric both nod and make their calls. My hope is the Judge did what I was directed by Chief King to do. I'm hoping he signed off on attempted murder for what he did to Lyric. We've both grown tired of fighting with the District Attorney on those charges. We feel they're necessary, and the more we think about it, the more we think we have a case to support it. We're also including the attempted murder on me and Mariah.

Paul hands me the arrest warrants when he gets out of the vehicle. "I ran into the DA. I don't think he liked that I went above his head with Lyric."

"I really don't give a shit. This shouldn't have been something we've had to fight for."

"We might get a negligence charge on it, Cap. I don't think we'll get the attempted murder."

"If we can get it on me and Rih, I'll take it. But I want him arrested on the three counts."

"Well, the Judge agreed with you. He gave us the three attempted murder charges. And he included the supplier charges, thanks to Blake's pictures." Paul straps on his SWAT vest. "You're going to have to face the DA, though. He's on a warpath. He threatened to fire Shelly for helping me with that."

I nod. Shelly is Paul's wife. She's also an assistant district attorney who has helped us get around her boss more times than I can count. If he could fire her, he probably would. Unfortunately for him, she's really fucking good at what she does. It might be the only thing that saves her neck when she sticks it out for us.

"Well, you know we appreciate it. And you know we'll go to bat for her if he ever did decide to make good on that threat."

Paul shakes his head. "She's too good of an attorney. She's worked as an ADA for a long time. She's batting a ninety-nine percent average of won cases. I don't think he'd dare fire her. He'd look like a fucking idiot with those others working for him. I think he himself is at about seventy percent."

I chuckle as I look around. Everyone is here except Quinn.

Matt leans against the back of my squad. "DeeDee is on the way. Quinn grabbed her a couple minutes ago. He was just passing her street."

"Good. Check the weapons. Make sure we're all loaded."

"You got it, Cap."

☆☆☆

A few hours later, after the sun has finally begun to set and we've gotten a lot of evidence about what's going on at Prench's house, I decide that it's finally time. This needs to end. We've seen that they have people coming right to their front door. We've taken pictures of them handing off packages of drugs and taking money in exchange for it. We've been lucky because they both seem very cocky. They aren't taking a lot of measures to hide what they're doing.

I take a breath before keying my mic. "All teams. Move in. No one gets out. Surround the house."

We're all in black. I know we're difficult to see, but we all move in from our hiding places quietly. We've been using houses around the neighborhood for cover, with the owner's permission, of course. It's hard to pull this kind of operation off in any neighborhood without the help of the community. Lucky for us, no one wants a drug house around them unless they themselves are also buying the drugs or involved in the drug chain.

Just as we reach the point of no return, two large, black SUV's with blacked out windows scream to a stop in front of the house. My heart stops beating like it knows exactly what's happening, but my brain hasn't caught up to it. I watch in complete horror when I see Lyric darting out of the bushes on the way to her next position. Blake yanks her back.

"Stop!" he scream-whispers into his mic. "Everyone fucking stop!"

I take several gulps of air with wide eyes while I watch four guys jump from the SUV's with guns. I realize all at once what's going on, but I'm powerless to stop it. If I send my team out without cover, we'll get into a shootout in the middle of the neighborhood, putting innocent lives of neighbors in as much danger as my partners.

Two of the guys kick open the front door. All four go into the house screaming and shooting. My heart slams in my chest as it starts erratically beating. I can't hear anything but the blood rushing to my ears.

But I fight it. "Everyone stay in position. No one move until I say." I move across the hedges of the house in front of me as I look in the vehicle. "Bravo Two, on me. Everyone else, cover us."

Matt watches me as he runs to my side. I crouch. "What are we doing?"

"Taking control of the vehicles. Bravo Three and Bravo Nine," I say to Lyric and Blake. "Take position at the back of the house. On my command, enter. Get to the front of the house. Block access back inside. Bravo Six and Bravo Four. Cover them. All Teams. Under no circumstances does anyone leave." I look at Matt. "Let's move."

"Yes, sir," he growls, laser focused on the SUV's.

"I didn't see anyone get out of the driver's seat. My guess is the driver is still in there. Go fast and hard."

"I'll take the first one. You take behind."

I nod as we both run in a crouch towards the SUV's. As soon as we reach them, we yank open the driver's side door. I'm trusting my instincts and relying completely on what I saw when the SUVs were exited. Two people got out of each. I didn't see anyone in the front or back of the vehicles, but I caught a glimpse of the drivers. I consider it a stroke of luck that they parked on the street, and the guy in the back got out on the street side and not the house side of the SUV.

We can all hear gunshots from inside the house. I'm doing all I can not to run towards it and take everyone out. One thing at a time. That's the only way we're going to get through this. One of my best qualities is the ability to adapt to changes and think on my feet.

163

Matt and I quickly cuff the drivers after throwing them on the ground. We gag them to stop them from screaming and bound their feet with zip ties to keep them from running. Not exactly by the book, but it's important they don't give us away. The element of surprise is a wonderful thing. We clear the vehicle, keeping our eyes on the drivers.

I glance at Matt. He kneels at the back of the SUV. I kneel at the front. All we need to do now is wait. It shouldn't be much longer. There aren't any more gunshots going off. Matt and I watch the door.

"Bravo Three and Nine. Go," I command as soon as I see movement at the door. The four guys start running out. "All Teams, stay behind concealment, but let's make some noise."

Matt stays crouched, but makes himself known. "Gainesville P.D! Stop! Drop the weapons!"

I peek around the hood of the SUV. "On the ground! On the ground!"

The four stumble, but as soon as the shock wears off, they do exactly what I thought they would. They backtrack for the house. Unfortunate for them because we're prepared.

A lot of voices start commanding the four guys to stop and drop their weapons. We all tell them to get on the ground. But it's not until Blake and Lyric appear at the door they had intended to escape through that they realize it's game over.

"What's up?" Blake asks cockily with his gun trained at their heads. He's using the door for his cover.

Lyric gives them a sweet as sin smile. "You should probably just do what the nice cops out there are commanding. Wouldn't want them to turn big and mean, would you?"

Matt snorts out a laugh as I crack up, but our tactic works. All four of them drop the guns and are even nice enough to kick them away. The team approaches with their guns drawn and places them all in handcuffs.

After they're all secured in squads, I finally take a second to breathe. I look around, but Mariah and Lyric are missing. After a moment of absolute panic, I see them both huddled against the house hugging each other. I don't hesitate. I walk straight for them and kneel in front of them. I wrap them both in my arms.

"There's... b-blood everywhere. It...," Lyric gags. Which causes Mariah to gag.

"Shh…" I kiss them both on top of the head.

"How did that go South so fast?" Mariah asks.

"Apparently, they pissed off another gang. Impeding on their territory," Matt says as he kneels next to us. He wraps us all in his arms. "You two okay? This is the first scene like this you've ever seen."

"I quit. Today is my last day," Mariah says.

Lyric nods into my chest. "I'm done."

I chuckle. "You know, I'd believe you. But you both love this too much. It's in your fucking blood."

Mariah gags. "Don't. Don't use that word anymore. It's stricken from your vocabulary from now on."

Matt laughs. "Then it's in your Kool-Aid."

Mariah swats him as she pulls away with a pout. He pulls her up with him and helps her away from the house. There's no way I'm letting either of them stay here. I'd prefer they head for the station and deal with their reports then stay here on scene like I'll need to.

I slowly pull away. Lyric looks up at me through her lashes. I kiss her softly. "How are you doing?"

She shakes her head and bites her lip as she looks down. "I don't know how to deal with what I saw in there. If Blake hadn't propelled me past Isaac and Ben…" She shakes her head.

I pull her back into me and kiss her neck and shoulder. "Seeing things like that is tough."

"I tried to be strong, but I can't handle that. There's nothing in the world to prepare a person for that."

"And that is why…" I pull away slowly and stand up with her. I glance towards Matt and Mariah. He's hugging her closely. I smile and look back down at Lyric. "That is why you are going to go back to HQ with Matt and Mariah. You're going to do your paperwork. By the time you're all done, I should be done here."

She looks up at me hopefully as I walk her towards Matt and Mariah. "And then we can go home?"

"We can and will." I lean down and kiss her.

"How are you two doing?" Blake asks when we reach Matt and Mariah. He stops next to us.

Matt pulls Lyric into him and Mariah. "They're okay." Matt kisses both of their heads. "Not the easiest thing to see, but they're tough."

Blake chuckles. "Two of the toughest women I've ever met."

I smile as Matt leads them away. I head back to my scene, content that my family is okay. While the justice I wanted wasn't served, I can't argue that it wasn't effective. Lyric, Mariah, and Matt are safe from whatever Hell that was planned for them. Me. All of us.

I can't help but be thankful that, though me, Lyric, and Mariah all had attempts on our lives, Matt didn't.

I don't care that Matt and our girls are capable of taking care of themselves. They're mine. All mine. They're my family. The pieces that complete my heart and soul.

Mine to protect.

Mine to cherish.

Mine to love.

Mine.

Epilogue

☆ *Lyric* ☆

(One Year Later)

A year sure flies. But here we are on Christmas Day, stronger and closer than ever. The thought of what we've been through since we all admitted how we felt and started this amazing journey always sends warm tingles through my body. What should have torn us apart only made our bond more unbreakable.

Mariah is truly in her element. Christmas is her favorite time of year. She always gets so happy around the holidays, but this year is much different. She has a glow. A glow I've never seen in all of the years I've known her. She truly shines. Sparkles brighter than all of the glittery decorations around the house.

If I'm being honest, all of us are shining more brightly lately. I smile down at the diamond ring on my finger. Mariah and I have the same ring. A beautiful princess cut diamond with tiny diamonds and blue sapphires on the band on each side of the middle stone. We also each have a band with diamond and blue sapphire stones. Both are on platinum bands.

They match the rings our men wear. Platinum bands with a blue line in the middle that spans the entire circumference of the ring. After the entire situation with Jackson and Prench ended, we all realized that we've been fools. We all knew that we wanted to be together. We spent so much time running around the fact that we all felt strongly for each other. We just felt too much time was wasted. So we got married less than two weeks after Jackson and Prench were killed.

The gang members involved were part of the Bloods. They absolutely didn't like the new drug running through the area and taking away their customers. Blake's contact was one of the gang members who was driving. Every single one of them were upfront and honest with us when it came to the CI. They all said he'd tried to get them to back off. He didn't tell them, but he knew that we were coming. He was trying to save his crew while helping us. Of course, the gain for him was that the new drug suppliers would be gone.

Blake still maintains that sometimes, though the CI is considered a bad guy, it's necessary to make the contacts. They can be a big help, even if they are doing it to gain something. Since Blake is one of the best cops I know, I tend to believe him.

Even still, his contact ended up in prison along with the other members of the Blood who were there. They were all convicted of murder or as an accessory to it. It's a terrible thing to say, but I'm glad they took care of our problem for us. I don't feel bad at all.

I don't think anyone who was there that day feels the slightest bit of remorse. We all know that while DJ kept us all out of the house for our safety, it probably also had a little to do with the fact that the Bloods were serving up our retribution.

But we're a close team. None of us would let him go down for allowing the murders to happen. He knew that just as well as all of us did. When it came time to write up our reports, all of our stories matched and made DJ out to be the hero he truly is. I have a feeling Chief King probably knew what none of us would tell him, but I really don't think he cared. He felt the same way about Prench and Jackson as we all did.

DeeDee has become close to us all. She's sort of like everyone's mother. She pops in just to make sure we're all doing okay. We have dinner with her every Saturday. We're all amazed at how things work in the grand scheme of things. Our lives wouldn't be complete without her, but how she became part of our lives is something that never could have been planned by anyone. The universe definitely had a hand in it.

DJ glances at me over his shoulder as I finish tidying up the kitchen. Matt takes out the recycling from the few presents we've all given each other. Including the cruise tickets I surprised them all with. We're all so excited to go in a couple of weeks. I've cleared it all already with our schedules. Mariah sits down on the couch and puts in a Christmas movie. I glance at the TV as DJ kisses my cheek.

"What did you think of the charm bracelet?" DJ takes the wrist I have my charm bracelet on and kisses my palm.

There aren't many charms on it, but the ones that are on it are very important. I love wolves. There is a wolf charm on it. There's a badge for our job. There's a lily because I love lilies. And there's a leaf because fall is my favorite season.

Mariah got a matching one. There's a carnation because she loves carnations. She also got a wolf because she loves them as much as me. She has a musical note since she loves to sing, and a raindrop for her love of rain. She was born in the middle of a thunderstorm. She was told her whole life that when her head came out, the sun peeked through the clouds. We've both vowed we're never taking them off.

"I love it," I say softly. "It's so perfect." I lean into him and stand on my tiptoes. I kiss him softly. I close my eyes with a moan when he deepens it and flicks his tongue across mine.

He pulls back slowly with a grin. "Ready for The Grinch? Rih's been looking forward to it all day."

I giggle. "Yep! Christmas sweets are on the table, and I just made a huge bowl of popcorn mixed with M&M's."

DJ's grin gets wider. "You really do love me."

I giggle again as I slip around him and grab the bowl. "Nuh uh! I love Matt!" I take off running for Mariah and Matt, who has just sat down next to Mariah and pulled her close. Just as I reach him, though, DJ catches me. I squeal.

DJ grabs the bowl and sets it down on the table as he swats my ass. "Brat."

I giggle as he sits down next to Matt and pulls me to his side. I cuddle into him. "Your brat."

Mariah giggles and offers us part of the big blanket. DJ tucks it around us as we settle in. Given the long day we've had today, I can't help but wonder if we'll manage to make it through the movie before falling asleep.

☆☆☆

I blink my eyes awake when my hair is pulled, and I hear a deep moan, not realizing I had dozed off. It takes me a couple of seconds to get reoriented. I snuggle into DJ with a yawn. He tugs my hair again with another deep moan.

I look up at him when I feel him moving. His head has fallen back against the couch. His eyes are closed. He's letting out sighs of pleasure and moving his hips. I shake my head, trying to wake up, and look down to one of the sexiest sights that I will never tire of. I'm instantly wet.

Matt and Mariah are double-teaming DJ. While Mariah sucks on his tip, Matt is licking down his length and sucking along his vein. When he makes his way back up, sucking and licking, Mariah switches with him, moaning softly. She starts licking and sucking down his length as Matt sucks on his tip.

DJ's fingers are tangled in Mariah's hair. His others are tangled in mine. I can't resist the urge to taste him. I lean down and start licking and sucking along his length opposite Mariah. I reach down and tug his balls gently as mine and Mariah's tongues meet. We make our way back up his length until we reach his tip and Matt's mouth.

We both kiss Matt while licking at DJ's dick. DJ's hand makes its way down my back to the waistband of my panties. When we'd all decided that we were going to settle down and watch a movie, Mariah and I picked out our favorite tank tops and decided only to wear panties with it. Matt and DJ decided on their favorite sweats and to forego the shirt. So when DJ's fingers find their way to my pussy, it's easy access.

"Oh…," I moan when he thrusts two fingers hard and deep into my already wet and tight pussy. He thrusts fast, hard, and deep as we all lick and suck his dick.

"Oh fuck," DJ growls when his dick thickens. "Fuck, I'm gonna come."

None of us pull back. We continue licking and sucking his delicious cock, taking turns at sucking hard on his tip. When he finally gives us the reward we've been after, we all take turns lapping it up and licking him clean.

Despite the fact that he just gave us a load of his come, his release hasn't stopped him from seeking out mine. He hasn't missed a beat in his thrusts. His fingers twist and spread. His thumb has found my clit and is rubbing at the same pace of his thrusts.

I have to look like a wolf in heat the way my hips are jerking into his fingers. As I lick his dick slowly, savoring every last drop of him, my pussy clenches tight around him. I try to push myself up as I moan. I can see Matt's fingers pumping into Mariah's pussy as he kisses her deeply and hard.

I whimper and look up at DJ. My pussy is pulsing erratically. "DJ…," I plead. "DJ, oh God. Please! Please let me come for you."

His hand that was just wrapped up in Mariah's hair, finds mine and tangles in it as he twirls his fingers in my pussy. I'm so wet I can hear myself, and so tight that I know when I come, I'll be making a mess. DJ tugs me up to his lips. He kisses me hard and thrusts fast and deep. I scream, but he swallows it.

"Come for me, little girl," DJ says against my lips before he claims my mouth with his again.

My eyes roll back as my body obeys his command. I let my head fall back. "DJ!"

"Matt!" Mariah screams at the same time as me.

My entire body trembles. My pussy quakes with uncontrollable clenches and pulses that roll throughout me. I shudder and shudder and shudder again as I ride his fingers while he thrusts me through.

But I don't get much time to come down before Matt is growling in my ear as he kisses me. He lays down on his back, tugging me on top of him. He thrusts his large and beautiful cock deep into my pussy as he wraps his arms around me.

"Oh God…," I pulse around him and meet every thrust as I close my eyes. When I open them again, Mariah is straddling both of us. Matt is licking her pussy as he grips my ass.

"Yes! Yes! Matt!" Mariah tangles her fingers in my hair.

"Mmm…" I lean forward and start licking her clit as Mariah rides Matt's tongue. She jerks into me when I suck her clit into my mouth.

"Oh! Yes! Lyric!"

Matt keeps his arms tightly around me while he possessively moans into Mariah's pussy. I feel DJ grip my hips seconds before Matt stops thrusting. I whimper as I tremble. I had been so close that being starved of my release makes my entire body cry.

But they don't leave me wanting for long.

DJ runs his dick from my ass down to my pussy. He slowly thrusts his dick into my pussy along Matt's, stretching me as far as I'm sure I'm able to. For a moment, I forget my own name, let alone what I'm doing. They drive me closer and closer to the edge with every thrust. It's not until Mariah whimpers that I remember my lips are around her clit.

"Fuck, Lyric," DJ growls as he thrusts.

"Holy Christ," Matt breathes into Mariah's pussy right before he devours her. He quickens his thrusts to keep up with DJ's.

My thighs tremble. My pussy clenches as tightly as my stomach. I nip Mariah's clit and suck hard. She thrusts over Matt's tongue and into mine. I arch when Matt and DJ slam hard into my pussy. They hold themselves as deep as they can as I pulse erratically around them and tremble. I'd beg for release, but I'm too busy making sure Mariah gets hers. I want us all to come together. There isn't another option.

"Oh God! Please!" Mariah screams.

DJ slaps my ass. I moan and jerk forward over both of their dicks. "Come. Now. Come now. All of you."

The command is all we need. I throw my head back and scream, coming just as hard as I always do with them. It's like my entire being is convulsing. I see stars. "Ah! DJ! Matt!"

"Matt! Lyric!" Mariah screams out at the same time as me. She comes hard. Matt takes all she gives him as she bucks into me.

"Holy fuck! Lyric! Matt!" DJ yells as he comes with Matt deep in my pussy, filling me until I'm dripping with both of them.

Matt grunts as he sucks and licks Mariah's pussy. "Mmm… DJ…. Lyric…" His dick jerks hard into me along with DJ's. "You taste so fucking good, little one."

Both Matt and DJ pull out with groans as I collapse onto Matt's chest. Mariah blushes and moans. Matt sits up slowly with me as we all pant. He kisses my neck and shoulder. I grip his shoulders as I straddle him. I can feel his and DJ's come dripping out of me. The loss makes me whimper.

"Tell me you want Mariah's tongue," Matt whispers in my ear. His voice is husky and deep. Dominant.

I pant a little faster, but not because I'm out of breath. My heart rate picks up. Butterflies take flight in my stomach. I nod and whimper. I do want her. I always want her. I want all of them. All the time.

DJ presses against my back. As Matt kisses one side of my neck, DJ kisses the other side. "Say it, baby. Say you want her."

"I want her," I whisper as I shyly look at Mariah. "I always want her." The thought of her tongue makes my pussy start convulsing again. Her eyes meet mine. They're dark and on fire with need. My pussy clenches at just the thought of Mariah's tongue.

"Such a good girl, aren't you?" DJ whispers in my ear.

"Yes, sir," I whisper back. "For you. I'm your good girl." DJ sits back against the couch and guides me so I'm standing. My pussy is positioned just above his head. I brace my hands against the couch as I bend. My stomach clenches with anticipation. My clit throbs.

Matt helps Mariah onto DJ's lap. DJ guides her down onto his dick as he pulls her close so her back is against his chest. I feel like I'm dripping. I'm already trembling. I look down and watch Matt thrust slowly into Mariah. His dick moving along DJ's as she moans has me whimpering with desire.

Mariah grips my ass and pulls me into her. She hungrily starts ravishing my pussy as they both take her. Every thrust from them drives her harder into me. Her tongue drives me mad. I thrust over her uncontrollably.

"Ah! Fuck! Yes!" I push down harder on Mariah's tongue. Every moan they drag from her as she tongue fucks me vibrates through my core. My clit feels like it's going to explode. My pussy clenches and pulses around her.

Matt bites my ass. "So fucking sexy," he grunts as he thrusts hard with DJ into Mariah's pussy.

Mariah moans and shivers as she takes them both. The pleasure on her face as she kitten licks my clit sends a wave of tingles through me.

When Matt and DJ moan at how tight she feels around them, it's like I can feel their pleasure coursing through me.

She slides her tongue into my pussy and thrusts at the same pace they are into her. DJ reaches up and starts rubbing my clit. With each breathy moan and growl that they all let out, I get closer and closer to my peak.

I know when she's close because I can feel her shaking. Her tongue is trembling with every thrust. Every nip she gives me, I can feel her lips quiver.

"Oh! Mariah! DJ! Oh! Fuck! Please! Please!" My pussy clamps down onto her tongue as I look down at her.

"Mmm… Come for me, my angel," she moans.

DJ leans in and whispers in Mariah's ear. I don't need to hear him to know he told her to come with me.

I watch her eyes roll back in her head. Her body convulses. "Matt! DJ!" She grips my ass and jerks hard into both of them as she nips my clit just below DJ's thumb.

DJ kisses her neck as he jerks into her and against Matt. "Holy fuck, Mariah. Matt!"

Matt bites down on my ass as he jerks into Mariah. "Oh my Christ. DJ! Mariah!"

All of the blood rushes to my ears. I can't hear anything except the roar that escapes my lips as I come into Mariah's mouth. "Mariah!" DJ rubbing my clit and Matt's bite makes my release that much more powerful. "Matt! DJ!" I claw at the couch as my legs shake. I try to stay upright, but I know I'm not going to make it.

It's then I feel Matt's arms wrap around me. He steadies me as I collapse against him. He helps me to sit on the couch next to DJ. DJ wraps one arm around me, pulling me into him and Mariah, while Matt stands and heads for the kitchen. He returns moments later with water for all of us.

He sits next to me as I slowly sip. The cold water soothes my throat and replenishes my body, helping me come down further. DJ helps Mariah off him and cuddles her next to me so he and Matt are sitting on either side of us surrounding us. Much like they do in our bed.

As we all snuggle into each other, Matt and DJ pull the blanket around us all. I'm reminded once more just how lucky we all are to be with each other. How long it took to get here. How ridiculous we all were to hide our feelings from each other. Being with each other is the best thing that's ever happened to us. If I've learned one thing over the past year, it's that.

I give a content sigh and smile when Mariah starts yet another Christmas movie. We tease her about them, but the truth is we'd do anything for each other. Including being subjected to Hallmark Christmas love stories. Neither of us would ever admit it, but we all kind of get into them, too. There's just something so magical about this time of year, but I didn't really see it until the four of us got together. I'd never known true love before.

And now?

I smile as Matt and DJ shift us slightly so we're all as close as we can be. I lay my head on Mariah's shoulder. DJ tangles his fingers in Mariah's hair. Matt tangles his fingers in mine. Their arms are tangled together.

I'll never let this go.

I'll never let them go.

They are home to me.

My perfect Heaven.

The End

Next In The Beautiful Dream Series

The sweet and sinfully sexy Beautiful Dream Series continues with *Crashing Into You*.

Home is where a person can realize and follow their dreams. Where they feel safe and secure. Loved. That was never my life in the United Kingdom, where I was born.

America.

Land of the free. My dream. Home. As far away from all of my tormentors and bullies as I can possibly be. An entire six thousand mile ocean between us. Gainesville, Florida, is a city where I can begin to heal from the scars of my past.

A chance encounter with the dangerously sexy Captain DJ Rens of the Gainesville Police Department threatens to derail all of my plans. I wanted to start over. I hadn't intended on the wickedly tantalizing, ungodly commanding, frustratingly enticing man to bulldoze my walls to the ground.

But happily ever after has never existed in my world.

When my past crashes into the safety of the world I built, all of the walls DJ broke through are quickly fortified. DJ is everything I've ever wanted, but I'm terrified of getting hurt.

Avoiding that level of pain might be worth letting the love DJ promises with his actions and words slip away...

Order *Crashing Into You* Today!

The Beautiful Dream Series

Available Now

Loving You
My Love, My Heart
Softening Lyric
Undercover Temptations
Captain Charming
Breaking Boundaries
Crashing Into You
Tactical Inferno
Ravishing Our Queen
Cherished By The Texan
Unveiling Our Passions

Box Sets Available

The Beautiful Dream Series: Box Set: Part 1
The Beautiful Dream Series: Box Set: Part 2

Other Books By Melony Ann
The Crane Family Series

Available Now

The Reluctant Mafia King
Sweet Lies
Billion Dollar Love Story
Be Mine
Protecting Her
Dangerously Forbidden Love
His Heart
Love In The Dark

Box Sets Available

The Crane Family Series

The Deimos Trilogy

Available Now

Connor's Legacy
Aryan's Alpha
Kade's Redemption

Box Sets Available

The Deimos Trilogy

The Forbidden Temptation Series

Available Now

The Detective's Forbidden Temptation
The Running Back's Forbidden Temptation

The Lucinio Family Series

Available Now

Rising From The Ashes
The Player's Rebel
Encrypting My Heart

Multi Author Series
Piper Falls: Firehouse 49

Available Now

Ignite My Fire by Melony Ann
Regain My Fire by Kindra White
Playing With My Fire by D.L. Howe
Fight My Fire by Darley Collins
Against My Fire by Anneke Boshoff
Relight My Fire by Louise Murchie
Harness My Fire by Ayana Lisbet
Quench My Fire by Havana Wilder

Let's Be Friends

Follow me on

Bookbub

Facebook

Goodreads

Instagram

Tik Tok

Visit my website
www.melonyannauthor.com

Subscribe to my newsletter and get a FREE never-seen-before NOVELLA
just for subscribers!
https://www.melonyannauthor.com/exclusive-content

Join my Facebook Reader Group!
Melony Ann's Sizzling Book Nook
https://www.facebook.com/groups/melonyannssizzlingbooknook

The official Beautiful Dream Series Playlist on YouTube
https://youtube.com/playlist?list=PLGEiD5wbQmDe1z4_FeeKbMLcBkOz
1M4L4

Dedication

You give us the strength and courage to live. We hope we do you proud.

Acknowledgements

Brad - Forgive me because I'll never stop needing or loving you. I'll never be able to be close enough to you or show you just how much I love you. I love you so much.

Laura - My love. My heart. My world. My strength. My breath. You hold me up when I think the world is going to swallow me whole. I would not be able to do what I do without you. I love you.

Jay - I know you'll never leave me. And in my heart, I feel you surrounding me all of the time. I know I depend on you a little too much to be strong when I'm not. I'll never stop loving you. One day, I hope I can show you just how much I do.

Anneke - It's funny. Out of every single person who started with me, you're the only one of that "warrior team" who is still around. Other than Laura, of course. That says something about you and who you are as a person. Thank you for still being here.

Jason - I hope you understand that I am doing a lot of things that I'm doing because of your voice whispering in my ear to go for it.

Kayla - There's truly something to be said about loyalty. I find it ironic that the ones who claim to be the most loyal are always the ones who stab you in the back. Thank you for helping me take the knives out of mine.

To the Bookstagram Community.

To my family.

To all of those who believe in me and support me.

To all of those who don't.

Cover by: Carter Cover Designs

Edited by: Alyssa Skaggs

About Melony Ann

Melony Ann began writing short stories and poetry as a child. She continued honing her craft over the years until she took the plunge and began publishing her work, despite having severe anxiety.

Melony writes contemporary romance stories that are full of suspense and a lot of steam.

When she isn't writing, she is loving her family and working to make her life something she deserves.

Melony believes that if her writing can inspire just one person, then all of her hard work is worth it.

Her hope is that her writing allows each and every one of her readers to escape for a little while. To dive into a different world one book at a time.

www.ingramcontent.com/pod-product-compliance
Lightning Source LLC
Chambersburg PA
CBHW071912220626
47052CB00002B/314